IRA WOOD

YOU'RE MARRIED
TO HER?

Leapfrog Press
Fredonia, New York

These are tales inspired by memory. Dates and places have been altered, events and characters freely compressed, exaggerated, and combined. In addition, characters have fictitious names and identifying characteristics. Since this is the way my mind and my memory work, to claim adherence to some absolute truth, however subjective that might be, would be impossible, and much less fun. As to the veracity of the pronoun "I," that is shamefacedly "me" throughout the manuscript and my wife, Marge Piercy, that's "her."

Portions of this book in various forms have appeared in *Ploughshares*, *The St. Petersburg Review*, *The Cream City Review*, *The Rowe Center Post*, and *Fifth Wednesday Journal*.

Published in 2012 in the United States by
Leapfrog Press LLC
PO Box 505
Fredonia, NY 14063
www.leapfrogpress.com

Distributed in the United States by
Consortium Book Sales and Distribution
www.cbsd.com

First Edition

Library of Congress Cataloging-in-Publication Data

Wood, Ira.
  You're married to her? / Ira Wood. -- 1st ed.
     p. cm.
  ISBN 978-1-935248-25-5 (alk. paper)
  1. Wood, Ira. 2. Piercy, Marge. 3. Authors, American--Biography.
I. Title.
  PS3573.O5944Z46 2012
  814'.54--dc23
  [B]

     2012019220
          Printed in the United States of America

"I am a monopolar depressive descended from monopolar depressives. That's how come I write so good."
— Kurt Vonnegut, *Timequake*

CONTENTS

THE SMALL PENIS RULE

One summer morning when I was seven years old, sitting next to my father in the front seat of his Ford Fairlane, I was presented with a question that would remain with me for fifty years. My father was a headstrong and self-destructive man. He held grudges so long he often forgot what had made him angry in the first place. He ate with gluttonous disregard for his appearance and his health, was disdainful of exercise, chain-smoked after each of his three heart attacks and died in his sleep at 62 years old as a result of the fourth.

In contrast to his reckless personal habits, he was the most cautious driver I have ever known and insisted on a literal interpretation of the term "speed limit." That is, unlike most drivers who regard the posted speed as a rough suggestion, my father saw it as the absolute extremity of rational conduct—like jumping from the window of a tall building at the first whiff of smoke—to be used only in the event of emergency.

My father drove so slowly it was hard to tell if the window was open. It was a common occurrence for him to lead a three-mile entourage of enraged commuters, his speedometer needle hovering at twenty in a forty-five mile per hour zone. Hardly oblivious to the furious parade behind him, the middle fingers jabbing out windows, the flashing high beams, the exasperated drivers bug-eyed with road rage spitting curses and pounding their horns, my father would initiate conversations with them in the rear view mirror. "Got an important meeting, Mr. Big Man?" he'd taunt them, or "Your time is s-o-o-o much more important than mine?" reproaching their audacious need to make the train on time or get to the hospital before the baby was born, always with the assumption that they thought themselves superior. As soon as we reached a broken yellow line and could be legally passed I would squeeze my eyes shut and hold my palms over my ears in an effort to block out the gestures and epithets from the drivers speeding by, because I knew we deserved them.

On this particular day, however, one car did not barrel past but came abreast of us on the left and slowed to my father's speed. Through his open window the driver looked hard at my father and roared, not a curse, but a question. "How'd you get that way, you little *putz*? That's what I want to know."

A *putz*, in Yiddish, is a fool, an idiot, but literally, a penis. Having been raised with my father's stories of growing up in grinding poverty (false, according to my uncle: their father was a licensed plumber and had work all through the Great Depression) and being sent to school without shoes (preposterous, according to his sister), I had a child's notion that my father was a strange and self-pitying man but not what it had to do with a penis.

Five decades later the answer found expression in a completely unrelated phrase, a naughty maxim from First Amendment law. Now the publisher of a small literary press, I was researching defamation of character in conjunction with a memoir we were publishing when I came upon "the small penis rule," a droll but practical safeguard against charges of libel.

According to the *New York Times,* Libel lawyers have what is known as "the small penis rule." "One way authors can protect themselves from libel suits is to say that a character has a small penis," Attorney Leon Friedman said. "Now no male is going to come forward and say, 'That character with a very small penis, that's me!'"

My father had nothing to do with law or libel but at the focal point of his mental picture of himself he was a naked man in a crowd of strangers, an object of ridicule and a failure. Painfully ambitious and hard working, a patternmaker by trade, a partner in a procession of hapless dress manufacturing firms in Manhattan's Garment District, popular with other men and, in spite of a serious case of acne in his adolescence that marked his face all through his life, considered ruggedly handsome, he was nonetheless handicapped by a loathsome self image and given to viewing himself through a distorted mirror, one in which he saw all his flaws and none of his strengths. Whenever his behavior reflected this distorted image of himself he did indeed act like a fool, a *putz*—and long after his death I admit, so have I. In fact, writing a book of stories mined however loosely from memory has caused me to wince on almost every page, to admit, That character with a very small penis, that *is* me. For the record, and those readers oblivious to metaphor, I would have avoided the subject entirely if my wife did not assure me I was of average size, an opinion as comforting as it is troublesome because I know how much research she's done first hand.

My wife is a prolific writer, hardly famous—fame being far too ephemeral an assertion for any serious writer who does not spend an enormous amount of energy in its cultivation—but admired by many for speaking truth to power. Considered too political, too feminist, and admittedly too unsentimental and class-conscious in her sensibilities to stay on any best seller list for long, she is, as even her critics would have to admit, an iconic American novelist and poet whose work appears widely in text books, rituals, anthologies, lit mags, newsletters, testimonials, dedications, and (almost the instant her poems appear in print, it seems) on the internet. For many years after we started living together we were something of a curiosity. There was not only a disparity in reputation (I had none) but in age, almost fourteen years (as it turns out, it is a habit of women in her family to marry younger men). There were many more reversals (maturity, education, sexual experience, success at earning a living) that, while commonplace between a man and a much younger woman, unsettled enough people for them to ask me to my face,

You're married to her? (Why you?)

You're married to *her*? (The writer?)

You're *married* to her? (Why would she want to do that?)

The answer has been yes for over thirty years now, but for the first fifteen of them, I admit, it was a question I sometimes asked myself. Why in the world would a woman writer at the peak of her career put up with behavior that was rational only to an albeit sweet-enough guy who was unsophisticated and self-defeating? This book roughly covers that time. Readers seeking insight into the creativity of a prolific American artist had best look at my wife's own memoir, for these are my stories, those of the very lucky young man she chose not merely to put up with but to love, and for slim rewards except being fiercely loved in return. They're the stories of a guy without a goal who took every half-assed, oddball, shortcut to get there; a guy whose guiding principle was the small penis rule, which we all follow at times, men *and* women, when our behavior sinks to the level of our self-esteem.

A Major Work of Fiction

When I was sixteen years old I fell in love with a mysterious yellow-haired girl from a prominent and affluent family. Knowing she was a year older than me and there was nothing that would remotely excite her to return my feelings, I told her that my parents were dead.

It was never easy for me to be alone with girls and with a girl like Allison it was impossible. We didn't use words like "aloof" in high school or "patronizing" to describe a girl who never laughed at boys who made farting sounds in their armpits but observed them with the detached curiosity due insect specimens, as if wondering how long it might take them to suffocate in a vacuum jar.

None of my friends liked Allison. The girls were jealous of her clothes. The boys said her ass was too big. In fact she did have more of a woman's body than a girl's. I loved the slow easy sway of her buttocks when she walked and the extra little twitch she gave when she knew some idiot was watching. I loved the way she crossed her legs at the knee in history and dangled a shoe from one toe, just biding time, as if all of high school was a stoplight you had to endure until it turned green. People repeated all kinds of rumors about Allison. That she did it with older guys. That her mother drank. But since no one had ever hung out with Allison or had even been inside her house I imagined I recognized something of myself in this strangely grown up girl: a weariness of things adolescent, a desire to stay beneath the radar of the residing morons, and above all a longing to pass through to the other side—to college.

At the end of junior year we both had roles in *The Music Man*. She was a Pick-A-Little Lady, a small singing part. I was the oafish Mayor Shinn, the second male lead. Because I had accidentally split the seam of my pants on the night of dress rehearsal I received an unexpected round of applause. When the curtain fell Allison absently squeezed my shoulder. "You were so funny!" she said, and from that one spontaneous gesture I had all the encouragement I needed. Summoning the power of positive thinking from a technique I had read about in *Readers Digest* called Sylva Mind Control, I offered to walk her home along the beach. Caught without an excuse, she accepted.

But I blew it as usual. I started to babble. "You like theater? I love theater." I launched long mindless riffs in a compulsive attempt to keep her amused. "But theater makes me sneeze. You know why?" She didn't bother to answer. Nor did she seem to care. "Because I only saw Broadway shows with my grandmother and her theater lady friends who wore beaver coats and feather hats and heavy perfume and as soon as I got in the car with them I started to sneeze. You ever see a Broadway show?"

She sighed as if having calculated she had another half mile to walk in the company of this simpleton. "My father's office is next door to the Shubert Theater."

"That's where I saw *A Chorus Line*! You ever see *A Chorus Line*?"

She removed a tortoise shell beret, shook out her shoulder-length hair and twisted it into a ponytail with an elastic band. "My father is the director's lawyer."

Allison lived in the only house in town with a swimming pool. She wore A-line skirts and cashmere sweater sets in winter, culottes when the weather warmed, and had a miniature Lhasa Apso named Cimba. ("It's Tibetan," she explained. "For 'small.'") She was an only child of parents who traveled everywhere, the kind of kid whose term paper described her spring vacation in the Fiji Islands. My family had recently moved to a four-and-a-half room apartment across the street from the boardwalk. When the windows were open it smelled of boiled franks. I slept on a convertible couch in the living room.

"You must be very proud of your father," I said.

"Of course. Aren't you proud of yours?"

A bland and predictable "well, sure" would have sufficed, but just that morning my dad and I had gone at each other again outside the apartment's one bathroom, the family *sanctum sanctorum,* the only place anybody could be alone. My mother sat on the toilet seat and cried; my brother locked the door to spread out his collection of Civil War memorabilia. The baby was left on the potty chair for hours with a bowl of cheerios and milk. My father went to the bathroom with a newspaper under his arm, a pack of cigarettes and a transistor radio, like someone leaving for a day at the beach. This morning I thought I might explode if I didn't get in there in time. "Please, Dad!" I rapped on the door. "There's only one bathroom in this place." I was doing jumping jacks when the toilet flushed and the door flew open. I had no idea what to expect. Since his last business had gone under and we'd had to sell the house, he was unpredictable. He might pass me by without a word. He might talk about me in the third person, have a conversation with himself as if I wasn't in the room. He rarely raised his voice. His preference was to try to extract confessions that enabled him to feel even worse about himself.

"You're trying to remind me it's my fault we lost the house."

"I'm trying to go to the bathroom."

"The *one* bathroom."

"Can I please get in?"

"Can you tell me something? Do all your friends think your father is a loser?"

"Of course not." I closed the door.

"Which ones do then?" he called through it.

"I don't have a father," I said in frustration. Allison stopped in her tracks. She had round hazel eyes with long lashes the color of white gold and she held my gaze demanding information.

"He's dead," I said, and for a moment I even shocked myself. Who even *thinks* a thing like that?

Allison touched her hand to my chest. It felt as if she held my beating heart in her palm. "I'm so sorry," she whispered. Her eyes shone silver in the moonlight. "But," she swallowed. She could barely bring herself to ask, "Your mom?"

Oh, what the fuck. In for a penny, in for a pound. I bowed my head. I didn't actually *say* she was dead but the implication was clear enough.

We were holding each other now as the surf pounded. "You poor baby." Her lips touched my ear. I felt a shiver in my groin and my legs were weak. This was an intimacy I had never known with a girl, never felt with anyone in my life. I had no desire to do harm to my mother and father. Their deaths were a kind of drama I was constructing as Allison allowed me to kiss the tears from her cheeks. Bits of movies I had seen, books I had read, comics, newspaper stories provided the details of what was becoming my first major work of fiction.

A sudden snowstorm. The week before Christmas. Just after midnight. The roads slick with black ice. They were driving home from their wedding anniversary party when their car was side swiped by a truck

18

on the Long Island Expressway. The driver had been drinking. My brothers and I were awakened by a plain-clothes detective in a heavy tweed overcoat. His breath smelled of peppermint. He gave us each a stick of gum. We were separated for months, sent to different homes, eventually taken in by my grandparents. But they were old. It was a hardship for them to raise three boys. We were finally adopted by a poor but well-meaning couple who lived in a small apartment across the street from the boardwalk and weren't able to have children of their own.

"You never got to say good-bye to your real parents."

"They died instantaneously."

"It must be so hard for you."

What was hard was establishing a double life. Because I could never bring Allison to my home—How could I be sure she wouldn't call them my *step* parents?—I contrived to spend all our time together at hers. Nor could I ever allow her parents to cross paths with mine or even speak to them on the phone. Because my father considered himself a failure he assumed I felt the same way about him and was resigned to losing a son, while her parents were delighted to gain one.

My presence seemed a positive relief, proof that their moody, big-boned daughter was not only interested in boys but attractive to them. Although her father had a Manhattan law practice that catered to famous names in show business, he was more than generous to a low-er middle class boy like me, especially an orphan boy.

He liked to give me his old dress shirts and cashmere sweaters and teach me how to line up a putt. A tall pear-shaped man, he wore tortoiseshell half-eye readers on the bridge of a long proud aquiline nose over which he appeared to view the world with an imperious bemusement. He was fond of squeezing my funny bone when he thought I was down, bellowing "*Nil Illegitimus Carborundum,* my boy!" and ticking off the names of famous orphans who'd become successful. It was like Allison hadn't brought home a boyfriend but the United Way.

Her mother called me "the Foundling." A sun-wizened ex-Broadway chorus girl with a cigarette-raspy voice, she spent most of her days at the club playing golf and evenings, whenever she felt she could get away, in the city, meeting her husband for dinner at Joe Allen or Sardi's, and leaving Allison to the care of Marina, their live-in housekeeper and cook.

When her father was detained at work I was invited to stay to dinner. Her mother sat with her elbows on the dining room table, tanned brittle forearms with sun spots, the wings of a crisply roast duck. She barely picked at Marina's pork dumplings and poppy seed cake, but made comments to Allison as she ate. "Perhaps we want half as much, Dear?"

"I'm fine, thank you."

"I wonder if Ricky would think so?" Ricky Fox was a favorite on a weekly TV show for kids. Allison told me they had gone to summer camp together.

"I don't really care."

"Obviously not." Her mother enjoyed watching me eat, however, and chose to see my gluttony as deprivation. "Have more veal. Pass him the mushroom sauce. I think those step-parents of yours are trying to starve you." She was full of stories from her days on the stage, tales in which she danced in rhinestone g-strings and was chased by a certain married producer who offered her bracelets and hats for, and here she would wink, "You know what."

"Mother, I think that's enough."

"The Foundling doesn't think so, do you?"

"Don't embarrass him."

"At least I don't bore him."

"I'm going to leave the room."

"When did you become so grumpy?"

In spite of their skirmishes I loved Allison's mother's stories of theatrical New York in the fifties, one big opening night party, one friendly neighborhood overflowing with the most eccentric and generous people in the world. Allison's mother was happiest when she had an audience. "Put another shot of rye in this drinkie, would you, Dear?" Early on she had taught me to make Old Fashioneds. "And a double dash of bitters? Good boy."

But when she was bored she could be malicious. One long rain-swept afternoon when a game of hearts turned to bickering Allison ran from the table and slammed her bedroom door so hard an entire shelf of antique ceramic dolls crashed to the floor. She wept as we knelt to sweep up the mess. "I can never live up to that bitch's expectations."

"Of course not," I said. "You're only one person. Your mother needs a roomful."

That was the first time she said, "I love you."

If Allison felt tormented by her mother there was always the presence of Marina to make a home. A large silent Lithuanian woman who lived in the maid's suite off the kitchen, Marina was suspicious of all male mammals that had not been gelded. She wore a headscarf tightly knotted under her chin and a crucifix the size of a Bowie knife. Marina doted on Allison, whom she had effectively raised, and looked at me like I was a mouse turd on a white lace tablecloth. Softly spoken, demurely dressed, Allison was in all ways modest in front of Marina, doubly so before her father. Having fantasized more about sex than ever having had any, I was happy enough with our long wet good night kisses and the occasional backseat feel at the drive-in. I loved Allison and felt grateful simply to be accepted by a family like hers.

Every year on the weekend after Memorial Day Allison's parents prepared a barbecue for their closest friends, retired B movie actors and former TV variety show dancers who took the Long Island Railroad from the city, no one I had remotely heard of, but who were openly gay and played suggestive games of charades and broke into Cole Porter songs at the piano. This was the life I might have been born to had I been lucky, the life I caught glimpses of in *The Thin Man* movies; the café society, the flip repartee, the urbane drinking, the cigarettes that seemed to punctuate conversation like a conductor's baton. I adored being included and would never have done anything to jeopardize my place in the family; then one day an odd thing happened.

Allison and I were in the pool. Her father was grilling porterhouse steaks at the far end by the diving board, her mother swilling drinks on the chaise lounge not ten feet away, telling a story about the first time she met Sinatra—when I felt a hand in my bathing suit. It was Allison's hand and it was no shy brush with temptation, but a determined attempt to milk the cow. Through the haze of Beefeater martinis and the rising smoke from the steaks, no one noticed. Later that afternoon in the pool house I tried to run my hand under her bathing suit and got a firm No! in response. But the following Wednesday on Marina's day off, while her mother was in the kitchen heating meat loaf, I felt Allison's fingers tugging urgently on my zipper. As her mother finished the better half of a bottle of Beaujolais and sang along to the original cast album of *South Pacific*, Allison stuffed her hand inside my fly. I told her about the empty cabanas at the beach club where my friends took their dates to make out. She had no interest. I begged her to meet me under the boardwalk. She said it sounded sordid. She suggested we do things that I had never imagined, she knew exactly what turned her on, but it was only when her mother might catch us. I got my first blowjob while her mother was upstairs watching *The Brady Bunch*. It may be that for the rest of my life I will associate cunnilingus with the sani-rinse cycle of the dishwasher because I spent many evenings on my knees between Allison's legs as she braced herself against the kitchen sink while her mother was walking the dog.

I was terrified of being caught, of being thrown out of the perfect family, but on the last weekend in June her father asked if I'd like to be his daughter's date to an awards dinner for TV stars in New York City, to sit at the table with the family and all his most important clients. Her mother winked. "We'll see Ricky."

Just some boy I used to know. A big jerk, was the way Allison referred to Ricky Fox. A freckle-faced redhead with a glossy pompadour and a lean, rubbery dancer's body, he was a fixture on National Educational Television, a kind of public broadcasting Mouseketeer. Nothing went on. Our parents were friends, was all Allison would say when I pressed her about sex. I had never "done it" with Allison, but I imagined Ricky Fox had. And the less she wanted to talk about him, the more I imagined.

Back at home my own mother and father were engaged in one of their prolonged periods of silence. They would occupy the same bedroom, stare at the same black and white television set while sitting at opposite ends of the same couch; eat at the same table, take slices of pizza from the same box, and pretend the other did not exist. Important information was conveyed loudly enough to be heard but addressed solely to the children, so that if I, or my middle brother, were not at home my father might ignore my mother and tell the 3-year-old, "I'm getting a colon biopsy tomorrow. If they find cancer in the polyps, my will is in my top drawer under the socks." But somehow the idea of their oldest son on live television awakened a shared sense of possibility, united them in a quest, and I became the family project.

My father volunteered to rent me a tuxedo while my mom prepared to remake me in the image of her favorite celebrity, an actor named George Hamilton, who had hair like Zorro and skin with the buffed polish of a goat-hide briefcase. As I more closely resembled Izak Perlman, it was to be a complicated makeover. A three-fold plan was devised. First, I needed a rich suntan. I also had to drop ten pounds, and lastly, my mom was going to straighten my hair.

Although the Sunday of the awards ceremony was a blazing 94 degrees, it came after a week of sporadic rain and unyielding humidity that spun my hair into a ball of grade 4 steel wool. At sunrise I spread an old blanket on the hot tar roof of my apartment building in an attempt to coax a fast suntan. In order to make up for lost time, my mother's brother Rudy, or The Idiot, as my father called him, also in on the project, provided me with a secret formula that he told me life guards used, a squeezer bottle with equal parts baby oil and iodine. Like a rotisserie chicken, I turned and basted myself every half hour. I did not eat breakfast or go downstairs for lunch as I was fasting to take off extra pounds and I did not realize the effects of the secret formula until I saw my dad's expression when he came up to the roof to get me.

"The Idiot told you to do that?" he said. My skin was scorched and raw to the touch, the approximate color of a red bliss potato. My mom led me directly to the bathroom where I sat on the toilet seat while she massaged hair-straightening mixture into my scalp. Then she wrapped my head in aluminum foil and moved me to the living room to watch the ball game while my hair relaxed. Phil Rizzuto, the Yankee sportscaster, was swabbing his face with a handkerchief. The infield in the Bronx, he announced, had reached 97 degrees. Allison and her mom were to pick me up in a limousine at five. It was now four-fifteen. My dad plucked lint off the tuxedo he had rented at 50 percent off, a winter model made of mohair. My skin was beginning to blister. My mom unwrapped my head. "Oh, my," she said with the expression of someone unpinning a diaper. "It must be the heat." My hair had completely lost its texture and dribbled down my scalp like gravy.

Half the building watched from the lobby when the limousine arrived. None of the children had ever seen a real chauffeur. An overly solicitous body builder in an ill-fitting double-breasted suit, he held open the door and softly said many things about my comfort. It did not register at first that he was mumbling apologies because the air conditioning in the limo did not work. Allison was wearing a real ruby tiara and a shoulder-less pink satin gown that made crunching sounds as she slid over. Her mother was rattling the bottles of the limo bar and cursing the driver until he raised the divider to shut her out. I found that if I did not move, if I remained motionless and simply visualized, in this case a water moccasin sliding across my foot, I could ignore the fact that my body was covered with second-degree burns. Relief arrived with a sea breeze as we swung through empty streets and even Allison's mother had gently succumbed to sleep. But soon we hit the Long Island Expressway, packed bumper to bumper with Sunday evening beach traffic.

Enveloped in the exhaust of many thousands of cars headed back to Manhattan, the long black limousine did not move. Allison's mother snored. My slacks, ordered a size too small at the waist to account for the weight I was supposed to lose, girded the soft flesh of my belly like piano wire. To our right a car full of teenage thugs in bathing suits, their bare feet sticking out the back window, drank beer and smoked pot and, laughing at the stiffs in formal dress, took turns spitting phlegm loogies at us. Closing our windows in this heat was not an option. I tried blocking them out with Sylva Mind Control. Think positively: Soon the traffic would budge. A loogie hit me in the neck. Utilize the right brain hemisphere: Before long, I will eat. I had not eaten in twenty-four hours and my stomach made those noises you hear in trucks that need a new transmission. Lurching forward a car length at a time, swinging into lanes in which the traffic abruptly stopped the moment we got there, we made slow progress.

The hand on my fly came as a surprise but Allison's expression was familiar, the one that always said, "Now. Now that Marina is washing the windows and my father won't be home until eleven, I want you now. Now that the chauffeur is blasting his horn and my mother is fast asleep and stretched out on the jump seats in front of us, let's do it now," and Allison silently parted the teeth of my zipper as we entered the Queens Midtown Tunnel.

The hotel was a Camelot-era palace of gold brick and white marble on Seventh Avenue. Allison's father, waiting nervously at the curb for the limousine, pulled open the doors and hurried us inside. This was my moment to shine. Born to a family of crass working people always in the midst of crisis, I was entering a world of women in rhinestone ball gowns and witty men in dinner jackets. The air conditioning churned, cold as a Moscow Palace, and Dr. Zhivago was surrounded by admirers. It *was* Zhivago, Omar Shariff himself, with a bushy mustache and eyes like liqueur-filled chocolates. Allison's father knew all the stars. Peter Graves. Carol Burnett. Mary Tyler Moore.

"Meet my daughter's beau." He presented me to Peter Ustinov and murmured sotto voce, "Both his parents were killed."

The great actor patted my shoulder gravely.

"He's our little foundling," Allison's mother said.

I grabbed a cocktail from a waiter's tray. Allison whispered, "Are you all right?" I seemed to have stumbled. Peter caught me under the arm.

What a question. Other than getting ready to meet the love of my girlfriend's life, the boy I had to assume she really loved, I had never felt better. The waiter offered more cocktails all around. There were chefs in tall white hats carving *chateau briand* and serving mounds of iced jumbo shrimp with silver tongs.

"You're covered with sweat," Allison said.

Indeed, I started shaking the moment I saw him, the slender young man with flame-colored hair doing an improvised tap routine on the dance floor. My skin was liquid slick. I was wet all over, but warm inside, the way you feel when you piss yourself in a wet suit. There was a gelatinous ooze on my upper lip which returned however many times I blotted it with a cocktail napkin.

"Over here!" her mother called.

"Oh, it's Ricky!" Her father led us to a cocktail table near the bar where Ricky Fox in a tailored white dinner jacket was clinking glasses with Allison's mother. His pompadour was like a wave in frozen motion. His skin was incandescent. The leprechaun smile, the arms outstretched like Jolson singing Mammy, announced not that he was happy to meet you but that he was happy for you to have the opportunity to meet him. This was what it meant to be a star, to radiate one's own light, to be the absolute object of adoration.

"Pinky!" He reached for Allison.

"Hello, Ricky." She offered her cheek.

"She used to call him Mr. Tricky," her mother said proudly. "Tricky Ricky. We all did."

"We're older now, Mother."

"Oh. Older. Excuse me. All of seventeen."

Allison was rigid. Uncomfortable. Standoffish. But not unlike the way you might treat someone you once loved, or still loved, who had never loved you back. "This is Ira," she said, and Ricky turned to me, but only briefly, as if one glance was enough. Enough, at least, to convince me there was still heat between them, that in fact she had loved him. Must still love him. Must have had sex with him. Must still want to have sex with him. Because he was Ricky Fox and I was, well, me.

Her father began pulling chairs from the table and I did need to sit down. The floor seemed to tilt as I walked and the band sounded far away. Voices melded and slowed as if stretching like taffy and the million glass beads of the ballroom chandelier spun above me like a dazzling roulette wheel. I remember prisms of lamplight, silver, white, then a thousand shards of color, a kaleidoscope of famous faces, as I fell to one knee and pitched forward. Allison screamed. Ricky Fox stepped away, shaking vomit from his shoe. I retched again and fell on my face.

I awoke, not in a seat at the round table for twelve in front of the orchestra, but on a king mattress with a striped duvet whose pattern matched the curtains, in a suite on the eighteenth floor. It was in fact Ricky's suite. "Make sure the ass hole is out of there before I get upstairs," I heard him say as two waiters carried me to the elevator. Hugh Downs was tonight's emcee. He told jokes with a puckish smile. I watched it all on TV as Allison sat hunched forward at the foot of the bed. There was a bottle of Pepto Bismol on the night table and an ice bucket with a wash towel on the rim. My shoes were off as was the itchy wool jacket.

On TV the camera panned the ballroom. The orchestra played the theme from *Hogan's Heroes*. Allison was sitting cross-legged, her chin in her palms, the blue glare shimmering on her bare shoulders.

Bob Crane reached for a glass from a passing waiter's tray. Fifty tables roared approval. I inched up to the front of the bed. I waited till the commercial break to explain. The sunburn. The drinking. The starvation diet. "I ruined everything. I lost it. I saw you and Ricky together and—"

"*Together?*" Allison sounded repulsed. "Me and *Ricky?* Ricky is my father's partner's son. I've known him since I was 5 years old."

"Do you still love him?"

"Love him? He's sick. He's a sadist. He always has been. He used to torment me until I cried. He played tricks on me. In summer camp he stole my underpants. . . ." She wasn't laughing at the memory, she was taking breaths in bursts, opening and closing her fist. "He put them on a baby pig, Miss Pinky, the camp mascot. We all came to camp with name tags on our clothing and when the counselors took the underpants off the pig they told all the kids they were mine."

Allison stood up abruptly, grabbed the telephone receiver from the nightstand and thrust it out to me. "Here. Your parents are worried about you."

"There's nothing to worry about."

"Why don't you tell them yourself? They're waiting for your call."

"How do you know?"

"Because my mother spoke to them."

"What did she say?"

Allison straightened her gown. She took a step toward the door and sighed, "My mother said, 'Hello. Are you Ira Wood's *step*-parents?'" and I saw myself as I appeared in her eyes, in Marina's eyes, the turd on a white lace table cloth.

It was over, of course. Everything. Allison. Her parents. Their parties. Their friends. I was no more than a family trivia question now, the subject of poolside laughter as the steaks sizzled and the drinkies were poured. What was his name? Allison's first boyfriend? The *putz* who said he was an orphan and passed out on the dance floor?

When I turned to look at Allison she did not look away. She gazed deeply into my eyes in fact and slowly shook her head and smiled, that curious and forbearing smile due high school boys and insects, then took a deep breath, stepped squarely in front of me and caught my face with the hard knuckles of her closed right hand.

The limousine company had sent a new car. The air conditioning worked perfectly. I sat alone in the plush back seat. The bar was stocked. Scotch. Vodka. Beer and ice cubes in a miniature refrigerator. Cashews. Peanuts. When we pulled up to my building it was past one in the morning. The click of my footsteps echoed in the deserted lobby.

I pressed my ear to the door of my apartment. Not a sound. I removed my shoes and turned the key, gently, gently, guiding the door to avoid the squeak. But the lights in the foyer were on, every one and every lamp in the living room as well. My parents sat upright, legs crossed, arms folded on opposite ends of the couch, waiting up for my arrival so they could ignore me. "Why does he hate us so much?" my mother began.

"He doesn't hate you, he hates me," my father said.

"But he told them we were *both* dead."

"*I'm* the one who lost his business," my father insisted. "I'm the one who made us sell the house."

My mother was indignant. "And I never account for anything?"

In a four-and-a half-room apartment it is rarely possible to be alone. Not when the living room opens to the kitchen, your parents are sitting on the convertible couch that serves as your bed, one brother is asleep in the boys' room, the other in your parents' bed. The

33

bathroom, however, at one-thirty in the morning, was mercifully unoccupied and sitting on the toilet seat with my father's newspaper, turning up the volume on his transistor radio and lighting a cigarette from the open pack next to the sink, I was enabled one deliciously private moment to ponder the roots of my problem while holding a cold wet wash cloth to my sore and swelling eye.

THE GIFT THAT KEEPS ON GIVING

My father had two major passions. The first was eating. The second was Lipsky.

On any honest list of the obsessions that occupied his waking mind, food would incontestably precede money, work, wife, or children. He could never remember the date of his wedding anniversary or any of our birthdays but he could tell you the restaurant in which each was celebrated and what every person at the table ordered for an appetizer. Despite his doctor's warnings and my mother's reproach, he blew up to two hundred twenty pounds on a five-foot-six-inch frame. After his third heart attack, he was wheeled into the hospital hallucinating. "The hamburgers! They're dancing." In the intensive care unit my mother told him the doctors had given him a death sentence. My father gasped, "Then bring me a pint of Haagen Daaz. Rum raisin."

Sanford Lipsky was our across-the-street neighbor

and my father's closest friend, his rival, his antagonist, his measure of himself. Lipsky was in medical equipment sales and although it would be decades before the Diffusion of Innovations became a popular sociological theory, he was the consummate early adopter. He bought every appliance known to post-war America the day it hit the showroom. A Tappan electric range. A Lady Kenmore washer-dryer. A Coldpoint refrigerator freezer. A Philco transistor radio. An Emerson Quiet Cool air conditioner. He had the first color television in our entire town. Lipsky was a swaggering Dean Martin in a middle-income suburb, Kennedy-era man-crush material. Broad-shouldered and suntanned with loose black curls and Ray-ban sunglasses, he wore sharkskin suits over thin V-neck sweaters and a diamond studded Star of David on a gold chain. He spent summer Saturdays at Yankee games and Saturday nights at the Copacabana, drove a Thunderbird convertible to my father's Ford sedan. At the time we lived in a modest cookie-cutter ranch. The Lipskys had a split level with a basement play room, a pool table and two-and-a-half baths. In my father's life Lipsky was the *ne plus ultra*, that which is ever to be strived for and never attained.

Sometimes I would overhear my father talking to himself, asking how Lipsky paid for it all. Where did he get the money for that? Do you know how much something like that costs? How does he do it? But in the end there was simply nothing to do but swallow hard and admit that Lipsky couldn't be touched. Nor could we touch the Lipsky children. Markie Lipsky took tennis lessons and karate lessons and played the guitar. His sister Michelle went to horseback riding camp and had her own pony. In an effort to find something, anything, to distinguish our family, my father took up bowling. Which Lipsky thought a great idea; he challenged my father to join a Sunday morning father-son bowling league. The pending competition gave me regular Saturday night panic attacks but the two of them managed to ratchet the stakes even further by placing bets on the side. During the semi-finals I faced a 1-2-4-10 split, commonly known as the "washout," with two fifty-dollar bills on the scorer's table, my father's and Lipsky's. With all the compulsive behaviors that would emerge in my later life, I can confidently say that any enthusiasm I might ever have developed for gambling was quashed on the day I pissed myself in front of a hundred spectators in a public bowling alley.

Although each night at the dinner table my father asked de rigueur questions about our day at school, he only picked at his food while warming up for the big one, "Anything new across the street today?" at which he seemed to draw his breath, to brace for the answer like it was a damage report. If there was no Lipsky news he lost interest. He was gone to us for the night.

The winter before I left for college my father salvaged an old speedboat, a fifteen-foot Century Palomino, in its prime a glamorous mahogany runabout. When he bought it, it was a barnacle-encrusted waterlogged wreck. He spent every weekend in the garage sanding and varnishing the deck, grinding rust from the hardware, laying a new all-fiberglass hull. With the purchase of a used Johnson 35 horsepower outboard motor we launched it on the first day of July. On the evening of the Fourth, as we were sitting down to a backyard barbecue, Lipsky backed his new boat down the street on a trailer, a twenty-three-foot Chris Craft Catalina with a 270 horse power inboard-outboard motor. What we took at that moment for a piece of charbroiled Keilbasa going down the wrong pipe was my father's first heart attack.

When I moved away I was determined never to repeat my father's mistakes. There were new worlds open to me, the most compelling the movement to end the Vietnam War, a milieu in which there was no role to play that remotely resembled my businessman father. I wasn't going have children or live in the suburbs. I didn't take the train to work, or have a regular job, or bowl. I didn't own a car. I lived in a house with six other people and three dogs, two of them named Che. The women in the house announced that it was sexist for the men to go shirtless during a June heat wave but totalitarian to administer a dress code, so they too walked around naked from the waist up. God bless the New Left. We started a food coop. We lived on brown rice flavored with *nước mắm*, fermented fish sauce highly regarded in the anti-war community because it was a staple of the Vietnamese peasant diet, but mostly used in the States as a liquid supplement for house plants. We offered shelter to the oppressed: homeless ex-convicts who helped themselves to our food and regularly robbed our neighbors—I once found a pair of skis in the hall closet engraved with the name of a U.S. senator whose son rented an apartment on the first floor; and pimped prostitutes who serviced their johns in our bedrooms while we were out. We wore used Hawaiian shirts and Harris Tweed jackets from Keezer's, hocked by Harvard students for drinking money. We lived in an enormous floor-through apartment in a triple-decker let by absentee owners who wanted no more to do with tenants than we did with landlords. Country clubs were unthinkable when you could spend sweltering summer afternoons in the park, smoking pot and tossing Frisbees to stray dogs. No one owned anything; the idea of envying my neighbor was absurd.

Yet as political discussions persisted into the night, fueled by hashish and jug wine, dominated by men who quoted Hegel, who not only won the crowd over to their arguments but disappeared afterward into the bedrooms of the women in the house, I burned. I was nothing like my father. I had no desire for cars or money or boats. But enduring the applause due some Marxist intellectual after a fiery political speech or blindly following a long-haired danger junkie with washboard abs into a phalanx of cops could trigger an irrational wave of envy that would launch me on an agonizing thrice daily regimen of stomach crunches and a hopeless attempt to understand nineteenth-century German philosophy.

Most writers I know are painfully aware of other writers' success. If you are anything like me, simply reading the *New York Times Book Review* can hasten the onset of gastro-esophageal reflux. If you follow the book pages you risk seeing praise for someone you've met at a party or a workshop; other clients of your agent or the newest darlings of your own publishing house. The movie pages are minefields of novel adaptations. Awards season, when Pulitzers and the like are announced, can send you into therapy. You can console yourself with the fact that the pleasure of writing is its own reward, and other such self-medicating horse shit or, as my wife likes to suggest, that someone who reads a glowing review of a well-known writer's book and enjoys it is likely to want to buy another book, thus expanding the potential market for your own. I can almost buy into this until I remember that this is the same woman who follows me around the kitchen trying to get me to eat fruit and insists that petting a cat for ten minutes a day will lower my blood pressure.

But I am convinced that these successful writers for whom my unachievable goals are within certain reach serve a purpose for people like me. They are not normal neurotics. When they write a sentence they do not stare at it for half an hour and then check their e-mail. They are not maladaptive perfectionists. They can read their own writing without experiencing stomach cramps. Their novels appear in bookstores every two years while I labor for nineteen months on a short story finally accepted by the literary magazine of Southeast Idaho Community College. Call them naturals. Call them Lipskys. They set the standards we labor to achieve. They make us all work harder.

In the last years of my father's life my parents had moved down South and my father was more or less confined to their high-rise apartment. He had few friends, no relatives with whom he still made contact, and as a result of his three heart attacks lacked the stamina to walk even short distances.

Up on the eleventh floor he spent much of the day staring out the window. I had the sense that we didn't have long together and on one of my last visits, attempting to gain perspective on my own problems with envy, I asked him how he felt, over forty years later, about Sanford Lipsky.

"Lipsky?" At first he had to search his memory. "Haven't thought about him since he was sent off to Wallkill."

"Wallkill?"

"I think he was out in six months."

"Wallkill is a state prison." I knew nothing about this. "Lipsky went to prison?"

"He would have done five-to-ten years if his wife hadn't been such a good lawyer."

"Ruth Lipsky wasn't a lawyer."

"Ruth died from cancer right after he left her. His *second* wife."

"Lipsky left the mother of his children while she was dying of cancer?"

"He ran away with Ruth's best friend. He married her just before his arrest."

"Arrest? For what?"

"Who remembers these things? Grand larceny or something. He worked for an importer. He was stealing from the warehouse."

"Sanford Lipsky?"

"He was reselling it all to some guys in Newark."

"That's where all the money was coming from? That's what you were competing against?" I could remember my father's young face as he hid behind the living room drapes and stared across the street, hair black, cheeks on fire, teeth locked in fury. All those years he thought himself a failure. All those years he judged himself against Lipsky's impossible collection of toys he was competing with a thief, a pathological narcissist who walked out on his dying wife.

I demanded to know, "Don't you feel vindicated? You lived an honest life, you stuck by your wife and children. You saved, you went into debt to put us all through college." But my father's attention had shifted. Now a doughy man with thin white hair whose once strong hands were as soft as old gloves, he was staring out the window, following the route of a mini-van slowly rounding the rotary in front of his building. "Tell me," I insisted. "Doesn't it make a difference to know that Lipsky was never better than you? That the deck was always stacked?"

But my father was absorbed in the scene below: some frail old neighbor being helped out of the van by an elderly lady, probably his wife, and maneuvered into a motorized wheel chair. It was the sight of the wheel chair that brought my father unsteadily to his feet. "Son of a gun!" He pressed his face to the window glass. "He has a Hoveround now? That's the Hoveround GT Power Chair. That thing can go seven miles an hour." He gripped my wrist with surprising strength. The muscles in his neck began to twitch. "Where did he get the money for that? Do you know how much something like that costs? How does he do it?"

The heat in his cheeks was back. His pallid eyes flamed bright blue. His jaw was clenched with the same indignation he had felt toward Lipsky. My father was young again and for the first time I understood how the man drew his strength, the pernicious life force that propelled him and that he had bequeathed to me. Call it my inheritance, the obsession that incited the father and, in his absence, would never fail to goad the son. Call it his legacy. The motivation that would always drive me in the face of overwhelming odds, the internal fire that no amount of personal failure, or success, would put out; as powerful as the force of life itself, my father's everlasting gift to me: the burning envy of other people's lives.

SATYRICON

1.

Everyone over eighteen thinks they can write a great book and judging from the number of manuscripts that used to arrive in the mailbox of my little publishing company every day, I assumed everyone had tried. Mostly people want to write about themselves, I think for two reasons. First, as with our fascination with the odors of our own bodies, we believe that the stories of our lives are intriguing and complex. But on an even more practical level, because almost every one of us has mastered writing in grade school, as opposed to learning to play the oboe or paint with oils or weave a rug, we believe we possess the necessary tools to express ourselves. I have often wondered, if we mastered ballet in the third grade instead of penmanship and were encouraged to communicate through movement, if the hallways of dance companies, like the mailboxes of publishers, would be crammed, as most are with manuscripts, with people of all sizes wearing legwarmers and spandex leotards, certain that no matter what their body type or formal training, be they hammer toed or victims of chronic inner ear infection, they had the tools to dance professionally. Nevertheless many people at one time or another in their lives try to write. I was encouraged to do so by a well-known writer who had read a play I had written and mistook raw energy for raw talent. I was flattered and arranged my life to have maximum time to devote to the story of a young man much like myself. He was sensitive. He was overweight. He had suffered. His struggles were intriguing and complex. I lived in a studio apartment near the heart of Harvard Square. It recently sold as a condo for $600,000 but at the time the rent was $80 a month. I believe that included utilities. I drove a school bus for a few hours in the morning and again in the afternoon, which allowed me the better part of the day to write. In short I had a situation that was perfect for a young writer. It gets better.

The writer I spoke of was also my lover. She was married but involved in what was called at the time an open relationship. She lived about a hundred miles away and would visit me in Cambridge two days a week and, because she lived in a rural area, we spent our time sampling the city's small ethnic restaurants and going to a lot of movies. Her visits were a holiday for both of us. It gets better.

This woman, this would be Marge, insisted that I was not writing drivel, that I had real talent and that I should continue working. On a typical day I would drive the school bus from 6 A.M. to 9 A.M. and from 2 P.M. to 5 P.M. and return to my apartment in between to write. On Wednesday afternoons Marge would arrive from Cape Cod and while I was driving the school bus she would read what I had written the previous week. When I got home we would make out furiously, critique the work, and go out to dinner, say, to a little Hungarian place in Coolidge Corner for Chicken *Paprikash* with poppy seed *spaetzle* and a bottle of blood dark *Egri Bikaver*. When we returned home we would fuck. Can it get *any* better for a young writer?

Marge's arrangement with her husband, although unusual by current standards, was considered commonplace in the seventies and merely kinky in the eighties. While the sexual freedom they allowed each other generated gossip, it was also the stuff of envy. When I told my friend Katie I was traveling down to Cape Cod to visit Marge, she told me: Marge Piercy lives with three men and every night she chooses which one she'll go to bed with. I distinctly remember Katie licking her lips as she spoke. Marge's life was an x-rated urban folk tale circulating around the remnants of the anti-war community at the time, but it did sprout from a kernel of truth. Marge and her husband not only encouraged each other to take sexual partners but made an effort to invite their various lovers into their home and treat them as family.

The experience that this arrangement afforded a shy young man, no less a would-be writer, was too good to imagine, even for someone who lived it. Although I had made love with a number of women, most had been as callow as I was and, like me, too embarrassed and unimaginative to instruct someone how to please them. My first live-in girlfriend, a whip-smart, fast-talking engineering student who was as close as a sister, nonetheless had an insurmountable fear of getting pregnant coupled with a gagging response to oral sex. A really hot date meant licking her nipples while she masturbated. My next true love, blonde and leggy, the daughter of a Lutheran minister from Kansas City, rarely spoke, barely reacted to stimuli; trying to please her was like flailing around a dark room, touching everything to locate the light switch. Granted I had more hormones than experience but I was desperately willing to please. Enter Marge who was hardly shy about what turned her on, who handled me like a sled dog, pure energy happy to be harnessed.

I had all the time I needed for my writing. I had a job that paid the bills and asked little more than that I show up clean and sober. I had not only a mentor who believed in my writing, but an older and experienced lover. Not infrequently we would travel down to New York City where we'd dine with Marge's literary agent and her legendary publisher. The lore of literary history abounds with famous couplings, friendships, salons, cafes, and writing classes, but surely my situation ranked among the best a young writer could experience. Could *anyone* be stupid enough to screw this up?

2.

The trouble with having the perfect situation for writing is that it leaves too much time for writing.
—An axiom

For you to understand this story it might be necessary to explain how my mind works. I create dramas, situations involving trouble and personal misfortune on a frightful scale. Behaviorists call it *catastrophic imagination*. It is as if I am only at peace when I imagine myself ensnared in some complex and tragic circumstance. If such a circumstance does not exist, I create it.

The other night I took in a movie. It was a tepid disappointment. Nor was there anything interesting on the radio on the ride home. Even the Red Sox were ahead nine to one in the eighth inning. Faced with a wearisome forty-five-minute drive on an unlit stretch of highway, I hit a pothole and imagined I'd run someone down in the dark. I had seen no one, of course, but the thump of the front tire echoed as the miles sped by and I turned off the exit ramp and circled back, not once but twice, searching the breakdown lane for a corpse. Finding none, I woke up in a cold sweat at dawn the next morning, checked the online edition of the *Cape Cod Times* and scoured the local news for days afterward in an effort to discover any unsolved hit-and-runs announced by the police.

So if a relatively tedious drive home from the movies is a situation intolerable enough to cause me to fabricate manslaughter, imagine the process of writing a novel. The countless false starts and dead ends, the months of solitary contemplation and postponed reward, only to be followed by the improbability of interesting a publisher.

In my tradition there is a story about a poor man who lives cheek by jowl with his large family in a tiny wooden shack. His children are underfoot, his mother-in-law mutters complaints, his wife is miserable. So he goes to his spiritual leader, his rabbi, for advice. Rabbi, he explains, I don't have room to breathe, what can I do? The rabbi tells him to go to the market, buy a goat, and tether it next to his stove. A goat? You heard me, the rabbi says emphatically, and come back next week. The man does as he's told. When he returns he tells the rabbi, the goat is shitting on the floor. My wife won't talk to me. It's worse! What should I do?

Go to the market and buy a donkey, the rabbi says. A donkey! But the man does as he's told and comes back the following week tearing at his clothing. The donkey kicks the goat, he screams. The children now have fleas. What should I do?

Go to the market, says the rabbi, and buy a cow. Not a cow! But exactly one week later he returns to the rabbi sobbing, pounding the floor in fits of tears. The rabbi shakes his head. Sell the goat, he says. When the man returns, he does have to admit, things are a little better. But the stench, it's unbearable, he says. Sell the donkey, the rabbi tells him. The following week the man is a bit calmer. My kids have settled down, he says, my wife is talking to me again, but the moo-ing, every morning at 4 A.M. Go sell the cow, says the Rabbi, and the man marches in the next time like a brass band. He looks twenty years younger. He's smiling from ear to ear. My house feels as big as a mansion! he sings. No donkey, no goat, no cow. Rabbi, I feel like a new man.

Moral of the story: The way to make your life better is to make it worse first.

3.

Sex is more interesting than writing. Writing is alone. Sex is connection. Writing is dry. Sex is wet. Writing is anonymous. Sex is attention. Writing is a puzzle. Sex is the answer. Why would anyone write when they could have sex?

But I only saw Marge one night a week and sex with someone else wasn't enough to make it worse. Marge was not in the least possessive and was in fact living with another man. It had to be sex with exactly the wrong person.

Wendy arrived in Boston on the night of a major snowstorm. She'd lost her job as a school aide as a result of budget cuts in San Diego. She had a young son and she had debts. There was a loan to pay off, she told me, then added in a nervous voice that trailed off as she spoke, that she'd hooked up with an escort agency to get them by. Desperate to turn her life around, encouraged by a guy she used to live with, she headed home to Chicago with her 4-year-old in the car seat of an old Chevy Malibu. But the guy never told her he was married, Wendy said, and her mother had a new boyfriend who didn't like kids. Remembering an old college roommate whose child would now be about her son's age, she made a last-ditch phone call from her mother's kitchen. Twenty-six hours later she arrived on the doorstep of the woman my friend Jackson from the bus company was dating.

Wendy was between jobs, betweens homes, between friends, between lives; she was destitute, afraid, a single mother in a strange city starting a new life from scratch. I knew little about her except that she was lost. And in own my way so was I. I woke up, took a bus, drove a bus, and took a bus home only to spend four hours writing nothing that had ever been published until it was time to take a bus, drive a bus, and take another one back. Marge's time with me was strictly limited by her own schedule and my only friends were a loose amalgam of people who had fought against the Vietnam War which had ended years before and who now fought with each about what to be against next. I was submitting excerpts of my work to small magazines and getting a string of rejections, doing readings in local libraries for crowds of six or eight people, usually homeless. Like Wendy, I felt invisible. When my writing was acknowledged by anyone but Marge a friend might ask "How's the project?" as if I was building a chicken incubator for the high school science fair.

Although Wendy was vain about her long slender legs and the dark chocolate hair that fell to her shoulders in loose ringlets, she was ashamed of her skin and used a heavy hand with powder and blush. Purple shadow made her eyes look enormous, almost childlike, especially when beamed wide on all the strangers she hoped to befriend. Along with bursts of inappropriate laughter and the short skirts she wore in the decade's coldest winter, she was clearly in need, out of place in buttoned-up Boston. Marge, by comparison, a respected novelist, a poet who drew huge audiences, an exotic deep-breasted beauty with the kind of classic curves that made thin women think themselves superior and their husbands think of sex struck me as an anomaly in my life. How could a woman that hot, and successful, and *married*, ever really need me?

Certainly not as much as Wendy, or Wendy's son, River, a ruddy little freckle-faced pepperbox bursting with curiosity and indignation; a fists-up bantamweight fighter with an eagerness to take on adults and bullies his own age alike. River was my first foray into fatherhood, instant fatherhood, and tripped whatever inborn instinct I had to nurture and protect. Wendy and River were living precariously at the indulgence of her friend Patricia, recently divorced, who was good-hearted enough to invite Wendy to share her apartment but canny enough to understand that living with another single mother who knew no one amounted to free and ready child care. So there was the rush of being needed and the opportunity to be a dad and in a time and place in which I felt invisible, I was suddenly the most important person in the world to a vulnerable little family of two.

But most of all there was sex. Wendy and I made love within two hours of being introduced, the week after she arrived in town, before she had even bought a bed, on a sheet thrown across the old living room couch. There was no door, which bothered Wendy less than Patricia, who was humping Jackson in her own bedroom, an event which frequently ended after a minute of thunderous bed shaking followed by the sound of Patricia's frustrated stomp to the bathroom by way of the living room, where she would sometimes stop to say, "Jesus, you people are still at it?" We usually were.

Even on that first night, before we turned in, Wendy said with earnest cheer, "If you want to put it in while I'm sleeping, go ahead."

Most women I had known desired a soupçon of foreplay at least, while Wendy's particular physicality seemed to preclude the need for lubrication of any kind. "Just pop it in," she might say, tugging her panties down, almost anywhere really, from the back seat during a drive-in movie to the lavatory of a Greyhound bus. Once, during a moonless night in July, a jogger tripped over us on the footpath surrounding Walden Pond. Many times I had thought Wendy would more properly enjoy a man with a much larger penis, something perhaps the size of a mature sockeye salmon. But she always seemed to come, quickly, with a shiver, like an actor downing a quick shot of booze before the curtain went up. Stud! Cowboy! Do me! she would moan. I had never had this effect on a woman before. But with all this, it was with her mouth that Wendy displayed a most singular talent, and while this would be an inappropriate space for any kind of graphic reminiscence, I can say I was reminded of Wendy just the other day while watching Animal Planet and seeing a python ingesting a wood rat.

Had Marge lived in Boston, had she not had a husband who, in spite of his professed permissiveness, begrudged our growing intimacy and my visits to the Cape, had I thought there was any chance I might be more than a part-time boyfriend, I might have buckled down to my book and ignored the temptation to add myself to mother and son, like milk to a cake mix, and cook up an instant family. But daily sex with Wendy was difficult to resist.

If there was one factor that stoked her desire to the extreme it was my bond with her son. The more time I spent with River, the more I acted the role of a father, the more games of whiffle ball we played, the more songs we sang, the more mornings I made him pancakes and afternoons I picked him up from day care, the wilder Wendy was in bed. Every night I arrived with another children's book, another VCR cassette from the library, and every night after River fell asleep we indulged in another debauch. *C is for Cookie. Bein' Green. People in Your Neighborhood. I Love Trash.* Most people I knew back then had hot sex listening to the suave bass of Barry White; I memorized every song on *Sesame Street Sing Along* and screwed like a porn star.

But it didn't take long to learn that the opposite was also true. Although Wendy had originally said she could handle my dating Marge, she was furious when I refused to break up with her and soon sex with Wendy was spiked with resentment. Frankly, because I had more than sex going on with Marge, because we, too, jumped into bed soon after she arrived, because we talked well into the night while Wendy and I had almost nothing in common, because Marge valued not only my work but my comments on the early drafts of hers, I decided the best option was to cool things with Wendy, to maintain a commitment to River and if possible transition to a family friend, when I fell victim to an obsession more destructive than any I had ever known, a hysteria to which I was all too susceptible but helpless to control.

It began while I was visiting Marge on the Cape, where I always made it a point to phone Wendy some time during the evening. Because Wendy was home baby-sitting two 4-year-olds and I felt guilty enjoying a good Bordeaux with another lover, I would go through the motions of telling Wendy how miserable I was without her, a charade she never believed but, with no other adult to talk to, she would grudgingly prolong. On this particular night Wendy sounded cheerful and vivacious. There was no TV in the background or squabbling children. In fact, I thought I heard a familiar tune. "I gotta go," she said after a few minutes. "Have a good time with Marge."

"You want me to have a good time with Marge?"

"Of course," she said. "Bye!"

"Wendy, wait. What's that song?"

"What song?" she said defensively.

"In your house, Wendy. The song I am listening to right now. Is that *Rubber Ducky*?"

"I don't know."

I distinctly heard the clear timbre of a young man's singing voice and above it the silly laughter of two giggling children. "Who's there, Wendy?"

"River's day care teacher, Chad," she said. "Why would you care, you're with Marge?" But I caught it in her voice at that moment, the answer to her own question, the click of realization—I was jealous—and the birth of a strategy taking form. "Gotta go!" She hung up, and all that night I saw images of her fabulous oral tricks, her throaty dirty-talk, and an entire porn film starring Wendy going down on some grunger from the day care center to the tune of *Rubber Ducky*.

The more lurid my fantasies, the more I craved sex

with her. The more she knew I wanted her, the more men she brought home when I wasn't around. After River's day care teacher there was the van driver, the cook, the director of the school, and then as far as I could tell, any guy who was remotely nice to her son. I couldn't very well ask her to stop unless I stopped seeing Marge. Nor could I berate her for acting out the very behavior that had attracted me in the first place. Sex was easy for Wendy. She knew how to use it to get what she needed. I was living proof. But sometimes I'd burst out, "Why are you such a slut, Wendy? To get back at me?"

"Why am I a slut? Because I have sex with other men? Is Marge a slut?"

"I knew Marge before I knew you."

"Well, I knew Chad."

"What about Teddy? Or James? Or Carlos, the guy I saw you making out with in the laundromat?"

"Carlos was sweet," she said. "River was cranky so Carlos bought him a package of peanut butter crackers from the vending machine."

"He bought your son a package of crackers so you started tongue kissing the guy? I can't even imagine what's in store for the kid's pediatrician."

Now, if I was reading this instead of writing it, a satyricon, a sex farce featuring a moronic self-absorbed satyr, the anguished rant of some fool complaining about an impossible situation that he had created for himself, I would say, Idiot, you have no right to be jealous. I would ask, Why did you get involved with Wendy in the first place? You were dating a beautiful older woman who loved you, who loved sleeping with you, who believed in your work. What did you imagine would happen? What made you think that a lonesome destitute single mother who fucked you two hours after being introduced would remain faithful while you were with another woman? Why would you go on torturing yourself?

Because I was writing. Because sitting alone in a room for four hours a day and attempting to make up a story is much less interesting than imagining your woman with a stranger's penis in her mouth. Yes, it is painful. Of course, it is counterproductive. But on any scale of interest or measurement of emotional involvement jealousy is to writing what five-alarm habañero chile is to cream of wheat. Writing is cream of wheat.

It gets better. But not until it gets worse.

4.

After some months I had finished a few hundred pages of a not very good first draft, but I had wild sex every day, some days twice, with two different partners. Wendy and I had reached a kind of shaky equilibrium, based on the fact that Marge and I spent only one night a week together when she was up from the Cape and their paths never crossed. There were the occasional complications that involved the application of

Nix Creme Rinse for Pubic Lice, but by and large, we co-existed.

Until one hot summer night, while at my apartment with Marge, I received a telephone call from Wendy who was choking on mucus and tears. "I'm homeless," Wendy said. "She's throwing us out."

"Who's throwing you out? Why?"

"Patricia, the bitch. For no reason."

Patricia's side of the story painted her in a somewhat more understanding light. Apparently she had arrived home unexpectedly to find Wendy and Jackson asleep on the couch. "We weren't doing anything," Wendy protested. But, according to Patricia, nor were they wearing very much.

Marge, always sympathetic to the plight of a homeless single mother, worked diligently to find a new place for Wendy, who eventually located what may have been the last available rent-controlled apartment in the city. It was unfortunate that it was two blocks from mine, and so started her habit of showing up for a surprise lunchtime date on the very afternoons Marge was scheduled to arrive. My sudden lack of sexual energy on those afternoons caused Marge to give me an ultimatum: draw limits with Wendy or she would give up on the relationship with me. Marge was seriously evaluating an offer to teach at a prestigious writing program where a former lover of hers was also teaching. It is certainly possible that Wendy's spontaneous lunchtime blowjobs could have been the factor that ended my relationship with Marge and changed the course of my life. But it wasn't; it was the fire. The electrical fire that burned down Wendy's building and left her without a home or an article of clothing to her name and brought her to my door one night with her son in her arms.

It had taken me exactly eighteen months to go from a promising young writer with his own quaint apartment and a sophisticated older mistress to a putz with two angry girlfriends who hated each other, a child not his own and, in lieu of a goat, a donkey, and a cow, an eight-hundred-pound gorilla in the bedroom.

5.

I would occasionally answer the phone to the following:

"Hi, is Wendy there? This is Brad from her Ed Psych class. No? Tell her not to call me back, okay? Tell her I'll call *her*. You got that? Under no circumstances should she call *my* house."

These were men from her night school courses, guys who were hoping for a little action on the side. Three nights a week Wendy was making up required credits, completing her BS in Education in hopes of getting into grad school for a Masters in Special Ed. It seemed like an impossible long shot, a single mother of thirty working part-time, studying for the GRE nine years after leaving college, but we rarely talked about it. In fact we avoided talking about our situation entirely. Our little makeshift family lived together in my small apartment along with the invisible gorilla, a huge and unmentionable presence made apparent the very morning after the fire, when Wendy opened a dresser drawer, found Marge's stash of black fishnet stockings and garter belts and threw them in my face; a situation hopeless to discuss because, as Wendy had no money and no other alternatives, there was nothing we could do about it. Therefore River was the focus, always. Getting him to school in the morning, making sure he ate breakfast, reading to him at night, painstakingly scheduling pick-ups, drop-offs, play dates; making life seem normal, making sure he wasn't crushed by the enormity of this love blunder of ours. With every spare moment, early mornings before sunrise, evenings, breaks at her job, Wendy studied. A teaching job was the dream, the only imaginable solution, the impossible outside chance that might ensure her ability to make a living for herself and her child. I could feel her sheer impatience with me, her excitement as weekends approached, when I might visit Marge and leave her to her son, her studies, her new school friends. There was no future for Wendy and me, only her present dependence, and the unspoken but mutual determination to see this mess through to a peaceful end.

For the better part of that year Wendy had a regular study group with people prepping for the Graduate Record Exams and although I never asked, and she never volunteered, I began to think she had met someone special. There were unaccounted-for hours in her evenings out, added care in the way she dressed for class, even surprises in our now very occasional lovemaking. One night, after never once having expressed curiosity about the position I have since identified as the reverse cowgirl, she straddled me while turned to face the opposite wall. It was lovely watching her ass cheeks quiver as she stretched forward, placing her weight on her forearms to climax, but of course I was left to wonder where she'd picked up this little trick. And then there was the night I arrived home from a weekend with Marge to find River simply bursting with news. "Well, don't you look like the happy little guy," I said.

"Oh, yes. Know what?"

"Tell me."

"While you were gone there was someone here." He actually winked. "And he was very nice!"

But mostly there was a sense of strength and confidence in Wendy that grew in proportion to her distance from me. Sometimes she would actually ask, "How's Marge doing?" and expect to have a conversation.

One evening in late April, she sprang from her car and ran up the front steps. The door seemed to blow open in a rush of wind. There was a radiance surrounding her, a shimmering aura of victory and newly won power. Her eyes were wild. She was taking gulps of air and holding her hand over her heart. In her other hand she was clutching a letter from Simmons College. She took a long slow swallow in order to speak. "I got into grad school," Wendy said, and she began to weep. It was over. Our ridiculous makeshift family had come to an end.

6.

That summer River went to visit his grandmother at her cottage on Lake Superior and I attempted to write again, tentatively, for an hour each morning, at the desk I hadn't used in months, in the room we had turned into River's. I was circulating the novel I had written and receiving the first spate of many rejections. Marge's agent, famous as a keen judge of talent, had attempted to be kind, but read it for exactly what it was, an episodic apprentice work seething with self pity, fantasies of revenge and imagined offenses. Wendy spent most of her free time arranging financial aid and looking for an apartment in a good school district. I took a night job as a waiter in a high-end restaurant and spent my afternoons writing something new, tentative sketches about the restaurant's spoiled and wealthy patrons, its petulant chefs, and the other waiters, artists like myself, unknown and hungry for attention. With River splashing away somewhere on the Upper Peninsula, Wendy living with her new boyfriend, who had been one of her night school teachers, and Marge on the Cape writing what was to become her novel *Vida*, I was alone, truly alone with my work for the first time in years, no women to please, no *Rubber Ducky*; no goat, no donkey, no cow, no gorilla in the bedroom. Rabbi, I felt like a new man.

If You Want Me to Be Honest

Located in the heart of Beacon Hill, the restaurant didn't serve food exactly, food you ate at a diner, but romantic descriptions of food, and charged by the adjective. Desert wasn't called pudding, however much it resembled it, but banana caramel mousse with Maine summer berries. An appetizer that tasted, at least to me, like a sour pickle was called a Kirby cucumber fermented in sea salt, spring water, Chardonnay vinegar, and Sri Lankan green peppercorns. At the time the concept was completely new in provincial old Boston, pioneered by a small cadre of ambitious young restaurateurs who were inspired by Julia Child's bodacious local TV show. Celebrated for our variations on traditional favorites—cod cakes sautéed in white truffle oil garnished with Usukuchi soy sauce and orange blossom honey; I had to memorize this stuff—and presentations assembled as delicately as a house of cards, we were among the first restaurants in a city known for Yankee comfort food to feature *la nouvelle cuisine.*

The owner/chef was Le Cordon Bleu trained and not only considered herself an artist but liked to hang out with them and hired a wait-staff of painters, musicians, dancers, singers studying opera, and me, the would-be novelist. We knew nothing about food, much less about wine, and blundered through table service with pure youthful chutzpah. Before I got the job I didn't have any artist friends my own age but the regimen of the restaurant soon made it impossible to hang out with anyone else. We slept until noon, reported for work at four, and spent the next eight hours at an all-out sprint. Exhausted to the bone at midnight but unable to sleep, we swigged the dregs of our tables' unfinished wine bottles, counted our tips, and primped to hit the dance bars while trash talking our customers, our boss, and all the undeserving artists who were making it while we were not. I saw precious little of Marge on her one night in the city as I worked Monday through Friday and arrived back to the apartment reeking so intensely of sweat, food, alcohol, tobacco smoke, perfume, dish water, and all the congregate effluvium of fine dining, that no matter how late I entered she would be awakened from sleep, sit upright in bed and gag. Every Friday night, however, I drove to Cape Cod for the weekend, leaving whatever bar at last call, grabbing coffee and a roast beef sandwich at Buzzy's, the all-night drive-in next to Mass General, and plowed the hundred-plus miles with the windows open and the radio blasting to keep me awake. One night I left Boston so blindly drunk that I arrived in Wellfleet with a sandwich in my lap that I had neglected to eat and could not remember buying. Much as I enjoyed the life I had to admit that waiting tables in a high-end restaurant, like working in the theater or the emergency room, the night desk at a daily newspaper or for that matter organized crime, guaranteed access to the shadow world of the nocturnal demimonde but made it impossible to conduct a relationship with anyone outside the business. I gave notice soon thereafter.

I had accumulated some savings to live on, however, and more than enough material for the novel. In a little over a year, I managed to complete and revise a draft that was competent enough to get me a good agent, which at the time I defined as anyone who had a mailing address in New York City, at least one client who had written a best seller, and took me to lunch in a restaurant with a wine list.

The book was rejected by over thirty mainstream publishers and although their comments ranged from the condescending ("Mr. Wood is a writer whose next project might be worth reading") to the absurd ("I cannot publish this book because I hate the protagonist. He reminds me too much of myself") I was aware of a disjointedness of opinion that I could not dismiss. Many people familiar with the novel, including some quite famous writer-friends of Marge's and audiences who heard excerpts read aloud, liked it very much. I kept being told how the book spoke to them of family situations they found painfully familiar, of what they feared went

on inside pretentious restaurant kitchens, and above all
how much it made them laugh. My agent had felt that
way too, at first, but wearied of making costly submis-
sions (these being the days of bulky manuscripts delivered by messenger), taking my lugubrious phone calls,
and building up the ego of someone from whom she had
yet to make a dime.

At the same time that I felt hopeless about ever publishing the book I was aware of being spared a confron-
tation with my mother and father, two of its more exag-
geratedly if not sympathetically rendered characters. It
was certainly the case that the guilt I felt about what I
had written enabled me to resist Marge's suggestion that
I end the relationship with my agent and submit to an
independent press, one that might have been open to a
quirky first novel, and I convinced myself that if I could
not write a book worthy of a big time New York City
publisher I did not deserve to be published at all.

Within a month of following Marge advice, however,
I received an acceptance letter from a small press located
in a remote village in upstate New York known mostly
as the home of a bar called the Rongovian Embassy, and
some weeks later the contract from hell. Never mind. I
was real. My novel was going to be published and if it
was to be with an obscure literary press this fact might
work in my favor. As an envious waiter-friend had said,
"Nobody's going to pay any attention to a book published in *Trumansburg*."

With the exception of the publicist, who loved it.

These were the days before e-mail, when book publicists prided themselves on their Rolodex, and I have yet to meet anyone who gave better phone. There was no Oprah's Book Club back then but if there had been he would have hounded her producers until someone begged her to read the book. He sent out an unbelievable number of advance review copies for a small backwater outfit and followed up on every one. The quirky novel from the unknown press was widely reviewed and not long after pub date I got an excited call from my mother. "Why didn't you tell me you wrote a book?"

"Didn't I?" Shit. Shit. Shit. "How do you know?"

"What do you mean? There's a big review in the Sunday *New York Times*."

But my parents only read *The Daily News*.

"Your aunt called from Phoenix. I'm going out now to buy the book."

"Don't do that!" I said. "What I mean is, a mother should never have to pay for her son's book. I'll send it to you." I thought I had bought myself about a week.

As family therapy was a term I had not even heard mentioned in my house, I'd never had a conversation with my parents about growing up. Like many boys I spent as much time away from home as possible. I turned seventeen, I had decent grades, I applied to college, I was out of there. I rarely came home for holidays. Why look back? Why tell my beautiful but vain mother I had felt her revulsion for me since I was ten years old when, on what must have been a very bad summer night for her, she entered my bedroom to say, "How could anyone ever love you, you're so fat." Nor did I question taking diet pills, prescription dextro-amphetamines, for years. We were always strapped for money. Doctors were expensive. They were obviously trying to turn me into a normal American boy. Whereas I now understand both my parents' struggles with self image and undiagnosed depression and can mine my childhood for its wealth of mortifying stories, in writing my first novel—the *bildungsroman*—the anger was still raw.

The egregious part of the book appeared in Chapter Seventeen, a totally fabricated first meeting between the protagonist and his girlfriend (read: me and Marge) and his (my) parents in a Chinese restaurant. In one of many similarly imagined exchanges the protagonist's mother, described not inaccurately as "a size five petite, an anorexic Madame Bovary who consumes no solid food except Sara Lee cake," becomes unhinged, not only jealous of her son's apparent happiness but his lover, who is a well-known writer closer in age to mother than son. Upon being introduced the mother asks, "I don't know if you want me to be honest or not." The episode goes on to report that the word 'honest' in my family is synonymous with 'vicious' and to innocently invite the candid disclosure of anyone's true feelings is to prepare oneself for the discharge of every sordid, unkind and spontaneous impression. "To be honest," the (my) mother extends her hand in greeting, "I've asked my friends and nobody's ever heard of you."

In the week it took me to decide what to do I came up with the scheme of using a razor blade to neatly excise the chapter. ("Damn publisher!" I heard myself telling my mother. "You got a defective copy?") Meanwhile the book was gaining momentum. I was interviewed on Fresh Air, planning a book tour. Mass paperback reprint offers were coming in. Movie producers were calling and so were the relatives ("You're such a celebrity you haven't got a copy for your uncle?"). Before I got around to sending the book my mother called to inform me that she had bought it. That she liked it.

"Really! How far did you get?" I asked.

"Chapter Sixteen."

I did not hear from her for some weeks after that and finally forced myself to make a Sunday morning call. "So Mom, what did you think of the book?"

"Oh, I got busy. I stopped reading it."

"How far did you get?"

"Chapter Seventeen."

"Is that him?" I heard my father's voice behind her. He took the phone.

"Hi, Pop."

"Hey, I read your book."

"What did you think?"

"Well, you didn't treat me too bad."

"I didn't?"

"But you really socked it to your mother!"

The conversation ended there. The momentum of the book continued. I was offered representation by the

William Morris Agency. A movie option was negotiated. But I now only sporadically spoke to my mother and most pointedly never about the book. Although I knew I could be considered a very fortunate young writer, I was ambivalent, and confused. Didn't the story of my own life belong to me? How was I to write about it?

My mother and I continued to have guarded, shallow conversations until in one of them, many months later, her feelings simply burst. "Were we *so* bad to you?"

The devil is in the adverb. How do you measure "so bad?" Did they beat me, starve me, abandon me; sell my body to strangers? "Of course not."

"Then why do you hate us?"

"I don't hate you."

"Do you think we *wanted* you to suffer?"

"You know what I think, Ma?" My mother was married at eighteen. My dad had just turned twenty. Her own mother was the most domineering woman I have ever met, a self-styled *grande dame* from the North Bronx, delightfully indulgent to her first-born grandson but imperious with her own daughter and impossible to please. My father's father was a semi-literate plumber, a callous and uncommunicative boor who took pleasure in playing him off against his older brother. When my parents were young, marriage was one of the few options open to children who longed to escape. Even sadder was the fact that they had not been in the least prepared to raise their own. "I honestly think you did the very best you could."

"We did," she began to sob. "Every day we did the best we could."

I'd like to report that mother and son reconciled then and there. I'd like to report a happy end. In truth mistrust still lingers and if all was eventually forgiven, much remains unsaid.

My father, it would turn out, read my book more than once. It made him feel important (or endorsed perhaps, in the way people feel about something or someone first encountered in the media) to see his life, however satirically imagined, in print. My mother became an avid reader of memoirs and began to send me clippings about books by writers who had also written about their families, more than once with a handwritten note that said, "Oh, what you did to me is nothing compared to this one."

Over the years she would refer to the time she first met Marge in that Chinese restaurant. It does no good to say, "Ma, we never went to a Chinese restaurant. It never happened. I made it all up."

I have taken pains since to avoid using my parents as characters, a situation that explains my mother's lack of interest in my subsequent books.

"I don't know if you want me to be honest or not," she once began by way of explanation. I knew it didn't matter what I wanted. "I liked them better when I was in them."

Mr. Nappy, the Artist

In my first semester of college, teaching seemed to me in all ways superior to working for a living. Academics had to grade papers, it was true, but only had to show up for classes twice a week, took long summer vacations, never had to wear a tie, and got paid to lecture a muster of scruffy adolescents who never listened to a word they said. Then I attended a sherry party thrown by the chairman of the English department.

It was held in his office after the campus appearance of a writer who had been his mentor at Harvard, a formalist poet of staggering critical accomplishment whose public reading made me ponder mortality for the first time. As an admittedly callow 18-year-old from the Long Island suburbs, I had never seriously contemplated my death, but his sonnets about Europe's monumental past, delivered in a resolute and dilatory baritone, were so dull that they seemed to suck the very oxygen from the auditorium and had me imagining what it might feel like to be buried alive.

I ended up at the party for the poet because my girl-friend was taking a class with the department chair. In those days faculty didn't mind students being around when they drank and in fact encouraged us to come along. In some sense we were like children, tolerated and ignored while the grown-ups gossiped, a kind of mirror of their importance. But in retrospect it seems to have been part of an older tradition of the academy: students were not to be treated as consumers but molded, exposed to the subtle lessons that could only be taught outside the classroom. How else were we expected to absorb the opinions, the hierarchy, the faux-British ac-cents, the costumes? No one in my family had ever worn a Harris Tweed sports coat with leather patches on the elbows. To me sherry was a song by the Four Seasons; I didn't know you could drink it.

From the office party we went to a French restaurant where I had the first classic *soupe à l'oignon* of my life. Waiters kept refilling our glasses with red wine and the cigarette smoke was as opaque as the conversation. The major poet sat at the head of a long table, a high priest in a thick wool turtleneck surrounded by acolytes. As they praised him he nodded at their well-meaning na-ïveté, squeezed his eyes and touched his forehead with a weary condescending smile; they would never know what he endured. He was doomed to be the "other" New England poet, he tried to make them understand, the second-rate Frost. "They love my work or hate it." He sighed and shook his great gray mane. "But not one of the important critics truly engages it, not one addresses what it means."

At the other end of the table, the less important, less populated end, where the light seemed dimmer and the waiters didn't bother to whisk away the dirty ashtrays, a young instructor had tears streaming down his cheeks. It wasn't easy to understand him, his speech was garbled with drink, and I had no idea what he was talking about, something called tenure, and that he'd never get it. All I understood was that he was miserable, the well-known poet was miserable, even the department chairman was miserable and, after graciously footing the bill for us all, tried to force his tongue deep down my girlfriend's throat while dry humping her against the side of her car, telling her, telling everyone within half a mile who couldn't help but hear his plaintive blubbering, that his wife taught at Bennington while he was stuck at a state college and she was sleeping with a physicist from Dartmouth. I'm pretty sure it was that night that I decided not to pursue a teaching career.

Some years after graduating, however, it was difficult to pass up the promise of money available for an assignment with an intriguing job title, Artist-in-Residence, as if there were grants for hanging out in my apartment. The theory was that the creative world of public school children, circumscribed by rigid syllabi and teachers who were at best well-meaning dilettantes, would be broadened by contact with working artists. Poets, in my experience, do particularly well at stints in the schools because children rarely speak in complete sentences anyway. Likewise dancers: how hard is it to play a CD and watch them twirl around the classroom? As a novelist whose own small reputation came by way of an autobiographical novel with frankly sexual material I doubted I had anything suitable to offer but was encouraged to apply by an arts administrator who assured me that children could learn self-esteem and advanced language skills by interacting with arts ambassadors who sowed the seeds of aesthetic expression by duplicating their creative ritual in the classroom. I was not naïve. I knew this was pure grant-speak and that I could not possibly be paid for drinking three mugs of black coffee and spending an hour on the toilet reading newspapers, which constituted my usual creative ritual. But I convinced myself of the educational impact of observing a real novelist at work, albeit an activity with all the attendant drama of a sea cow grazing in a shallow Florida river.

Getting the job would not be easy. The pay was first rate at the time, more than double what I made waiting tables, but the interview was like a cut-throat gong show for desperate MFAs. Here were dancers in leotards, a slam poet in a *dashiki*, and a cowboy songwriter with a harmonica and guitar; a photographer in a khaki safari vest and bush hat, a storyteller with a cockatoo on his shoulder, and a basket weaver from Nantucket with a leather bagful of black ash splints. With five minutes allotted each applicant I knew from the start I hadn't a chance. I had drawn number twenty-two and took the stage only to stare into the weary faces of fifty school principals stealing glances at their watches. I couldn't have pleased them more than if I'd screamed *Fire!* and given us all an excuse to bolt. With that in mind, I didn't read the piece I had prepared, an insipid story about my cat that in itself begged the issue of my suitability for a job in the schools—his name was Jim Beam—and resigned myself to a quick exit. "I've written some plays," I said, "I'm working on my second novel now. My first one was published by a small press but we did sell the movie rights to Universal." I immediately sensed a sudden stirring, a faint invigoration of interest. "My agent is working on a deal for me to write the screenplay."

They began shuffling forward in order to hear. Some even raised their hands with questions. It was as if fifty glazed doughnuts became faces with eyes and ears. It took me a moment to comprehend the change, but the other artists understood. Their expressions cried, Unfair! I hadn't pretended to any expertise in working with children, as had been the strategy of their dog-and-pony shows, but accidently connected with the fantasies of the people who did the hiring. Ambitious bureaucrats whose careers doomed them to remain in public school forever, they unexpectedly had a chance to work with someone who had an agent. "Who's going to star in the movie?" one principal wanted to know, while another cornered me in the men's room: "Do you think you could get a script to Scorsese?"

After a spirited competition for my services, I was assigned to a vocational technical high school in a decaying industrial city north of Boston where, according to the buzz of the arts administrators, someone like me "could really make a difference."

Apparently not to the office secretary, who did not lift her eyes from her keyboard on the morning of my first class but called over her shoulder to the assistant principal, who sneered at my jacket and tie and walked past me without a word. His name was Mr. Burger, pronounced, in the Boston area, Bur-GAH. Five-foot-four inches tall with a nose like a red bell pepper and a shaved head, he wore a black turtleneck with rolled-up sleeves and swung his forearms like nightsticks.

"I picked up some newspapers on the way to school," I said when I caught him looking at the stack under my arm. In truth I'd planned to kill some time with them in a toilet stall, but a glance at my schedule showed classes back to back. "I thought the students and I might read them together and talk about what constitutes a narrative."

"Did you say *read*?" I had apparently given Mr. Bur-GAH his second good laugh of the day. His first had been my hair, which I wore in what was called an afro in those days, a large frizzy brown bush the shape of a Tootsie Roll lollipop, but mostly he ignored me, scanning the halls as he walked, like a camera over a bank teller's shoulder. "Just try to keep 'em in the room till the bell rings."

He stood in the classroom doorway as nineteen students made their way to their desks as slowly as was humanly possible. "This is Mr. Wood," he said.

"Looks like Mr. Nappy-head to me," one student said. "Where you get your hair cut, Nappy?"

"You mean lawn-mowed," offered another.

"Should we broil him or fry him, Mr. Bur-GAH?"

A flicker of mischief lit the vice principal's eyes and his emerging smile built anticipation like a drum roll. "Have it your way!" He beamed at the spontaneous outpouring of laughter and high-fives. As he turned to leave he handed me a class list and checked his watch with a theatrical flourish, betting on how long I'd last.

There are students who completely ignore you, who remain collectively deaf to your best intentions and repel your carefully prepared plans. There are students who groan with every request you make, however logical or mundane, and others who gape, as if they had never seen anything remotely like you, as if you were a creature so alien to their experience that you did not register as human.

This class didn't look at me at all, but at each other, dead expressions come alive with sadistic possibility. I felt like the watchman in *A Night at the Museum* as the T. Rex and the Civil War mannequins advanced in a conspiracy to send me screaming down the escalator steps.

When in doubt take attendance. "Carbo, Peter S." I said.

"Fuck you," said a kid in the front row. He wore sneakers the size of anti-gravity boots and sat in the position commonly assumed for a pelvic exam.

"Knott, Daniel. Just say Here, please."

Mr. Knott pointed to his crotch. "Here, please."

"Munson, Robert." No answer.

"Henry Turturo?" No answer. ". . . called Robert Munson's mother a meat head."

A chair flew back. "You said that?"

The accusation was angrily refuted. "Did fucking not!"

I checked them off. "Turturo, here. Munson, here."

Sneakers liked that. "Pretty good, Nappy."

"Pinola, Bruce?"

Now they were on their guard.

"Did you know Pinola means condom in Spanish?"

"Fuck you it does," said a voice in the second row.

"Good morning, Mr. Pinola." Following the filthiest exchange of language ever induced by the taking of attendance, we buckled down to the day's lesson, an improvised version of my original plan, which now involved a dramatic reading of the comic strips.

Mr. Bur-GAH was peaking into the classroom as the bell rang and I was struck by his resemblance to Uncle Fester of the Addams Family. He gave me an astonished thumbs-up as all nineteen students passed from the room in good humor.

Bruce Pinola said, "You gonna be here tomorrow, Nappy?"

"Mr. Nappy to you," I corrected him.

"We love this guy, Mr. Bur-GAH."

Carbo, the sneaker man, was also enthused. "Tomorrow I'm bein' Garfield."

Word spread. Kids flocked to my classes to be insulted during attendance and vie to play John the Turtle and the Dookie Bird. As I headed down the hallway for lunch, Mr. Bur-GAH slipped his fist under my armpit and steered me into the teachers' lounge with an affectionate half nelson, a fetid yellow closet of a room crowded with twelve wax-like figures around a Formica table.

"This is Nappy, the artist." Mr. Bur-GAH announced. "He kicked ass this morning."

One bloodless face looked up with a mouthful of egg salad on white. "They're tenth graders," he said. "Let's see how he does with the seniors this afternoon."

"Jerk-off," Mr. Bur-GAH mumbled. "Don't listen to him." He punctuated his admonition with an index finger in my solar plexus. "Listen, after you get settled in I want to talk to you about this idea I have about a mini-series set in a high school."

In the course of my career as an artist in the schools I have been required to teach classes from kindergarten to twelfth grade, to serve school lunches, to supervise after-school detention. I have produced a circus and a musical revue with a former composer for Saturday Night Live, adapted classics as plays to be performed by children who could not read, and invented game shows. I have organized student-teacher conga lines, choreographed dances with special needs students, conducted radio interviews with household pets, and filmed an 8 mm movie about making Jell-o. My most popular turn by far was the invention of Dr. Memory.

Frantic one morning for some trick, however bizarre, to amuse the jaded students of a suburban middle school in an affluent suburb north of Providence, I loaded a shoebox with natural flavor extracts off the kitchen spice rack. Vanilla, grapefruit, watermelon, pomegranate, wheat grass, there were twenty-eight of them in all. My act involved wearing a turban (read: beach towel), blindfolding the students and waving a bottle of extract under their noses while asking them where they were being transported in their minds, and then of course making them write about it. The first classes were difficult, the most skeptical students resistant.

"Yuch puke! Get that out of my nose."

"The girl before me had boogers!"

"It tickles. You're making me sneeze."

The next day, however, I brought in extra towels and turned the troublemakers into my assistants. I added a boom box to the act, playing one of my wife's belly dancing tapes. With a little encouragement they were dreaming themselves back to early childhood, to family vacations, and writing about the cities in which their grandparents were born. Every class wanted a visit from Dr. Memory.

In six years as an artist-in-residence, however, I could

not do one stitch of my own work during any semester in which I was working in the schools. My time off was spent recovering my self-image and my inner strength, self-medicating and amassing ever more *schtick* so as not to be eaten alive in the classroom. I am more than incredulous that some of our country's favorite writers have a thriving teaching career and I have no idea how they do it. In the limited times I have taught on the college level, my students' family problems, their bad habits, idiotic decisions, and insulting opinions, not to mention the demands of reading and evaluating their work, have preempted all my energy for writing. The sensitivity needed to say something positive to a puerile and sentimental childhood story; the facility to encourage the one talented writer in the class while remaining mindful of the feelings of the duds; the discipline required to stop myself from rewriting their crap entirely; the tact not to question their choice to become a writer at all; the requisite soundness of mind to admit to myself that any winsome 20-year-old who follows me around like a puppy and tells me my work changed her life is probably under psychiatric care and most assuredly trouble; in short all the psychological heavy lifting that does not appear on the syllabus but is incumbent on a good teacher, exhausted the same limited supply of emotional energy I had for my own work.

I made good money as an artist in the schools and had no shortage of assignments but eventually returned to the grinding anonymity of restaurant work. I wasn't teaching them how to be fiction writers, or even, like the poets and dancers and photographers, imparting a watered down version of my trade. I was just an entertainer, a birthday party clown, a kind of Bozo-the-Artist who came into their classes with a new act every week. Frankly, I felt like a fraud.

Although once, decades later, a balding man in his thirties stopped me on the street. "Hey wait!" He had a little girl in hand, probably his daughter, and he ran up to me excitedly. "Weren't you the guy who came into my classroom one day with a shoebox full of flavor extracts?" I admitted that I was. "That was so cool, man," he said to his daughter. "That was one of the only cool things that ever happened in school. What's your name again?"

I was surprised to find myself reacting with no small measure of pride. "Why, Mr. Nappy, the artist."

A Work in F**king Progress

1.

In the autumn of the year I turned 30 years old Ronald Reagan was elected president, a right-wing working majority overtook both houses of congress, and Marge's husband returned from a Caribbean vacation to announce that he was getting his vasectomy reversed and wanted a divorce. As the country embraced core family values, Marge and I, in practice if not by design, were suddenly a traditional monogamous couple, splitting our time between her house on Cape Cod and a cheap but enormous apartment in Cambridge, taking a family membership at the food co-op, acquiring two kittens, dividing kitchen chores, and hunkering down every day to write.

Some four years before, I had contrived to meet Marge when my upstairs neighbor announced, coincidently on the afternoon of the first Passover Seder, that a notorious writer friend was coming to visit. *Woman on the Edge of Time*, now a sci-fi classic, had just been released, and before that, *Small Changes* and *Dance the Eagle to Sleep*, both bibles of the New Left. In a photograph I had seen in *Time* magazine, Marge Piercy, with severe black bangs, a cigarette pursed in Gallic lips, looked like a French movie star. Because I couldn't imagine what I might say upon being introduced, I interrupted their conversation with a kind of impromptu performance piece, appearing with a bowl of egg whites while attempting to whip them with a wire whisk. Nine out of ten successful women would have written me off as some incompetent busybody trying to make macaroons; Marge saw a profile from JDate: 26-year-old Jewish man, curly hair, likes to cook.

Marge received all kinds of flack from women friends and feminist intellectuals. He'll leave her when she gets old, was the common wisdom. "Toy Boy" was a phrase directed at me more than once, and my favorite, overheard from a semiotician at a communication theory conference, "Big hair, big sex." But we seemed to click as well as any serious woman writer at the height of her fame could with a shallow young man fourteen years her junior.

Marge's novels were bringing in six-figure advances. Lucrative speaking engagements kept her on the road. After a contentious divorce, she had managed to keep the house. I was pleased with the progress of a new book I had begun. Life was good, unfortunately too good, a situation that always upset my inner balance, made me feel undeserving and caused me, however unconsciously, to seek a return to a more uncomfortable level: to set things right again, or in my case, wrong.

2.

As the humid dregs of the long hot summer surrendered to a classic New England fall, Marge was off on a four-day gig in the Midwest. Disinclined to spend yet another weekend alone, I decided to take a scenic drive to visit an old friend in Vermont. When I had seen her last, Karen had been in an abusive marriage. Late one afternoon she casually strolled into the living room, told her husband she was going to the corner store for cigarettes, reminded him that one of his favorites, shepherd's pie, was in the oven, herded her two young children into her previously packed station wagon, and disappeared. Some years later she surfaced with a new address, a new career, and a new name, Kharma Mountainchild, in a small town just south of Rutland.

We had a pizza on the night I arrived and watched TV on her bed with the kids. She put them to sleep and we drank a little wine. Although we had not been friends for long we had shared many secrets, having been partners in a popular lay psychotherapy movement called Re-evaluation Counseling, one in which we took turns as counselor and client. Chief among the rules—listen without interrupting, never make judgments, etc.—was that partners could never have sex. There was really no reason then to ask her to take her head off my shoulder.

Did I want to smoke a joint? Kharma asked. Why not? Would I roll it while she went to the bathroom? No problem. And upon returning to the bedroom naked except for a black lace bra, Didn't I always really want to do this? I suppose I had.

Throughout the course of my much younger life I have had occasion to observe that whenever I had *not* been looking for sex, had no particular desire, no attraction, no place to do it or time to do it in, the opportunity often arose unbidden. Like the very next night back in Boston at the restaurant where I worked, when a waitress with whom I'd been carrying on a mild flirtation abruptly announced she had lost her apartment and was moving west. Could she buy me a farewell drink? Of course. Could I put her up at my place? Why not? The sex was entirely forgettable, a fumbling late night attempt to create closure to a connection that was a fantasy to begin with. It led to nothing. In fact I divulged everything upon Marge's return. I don't think we had left the baggage carousel at Logan airport before I begged forgiveness. I swore fidelity forever. End of story.

Except that a few days later, while on the Cape, I began to feel caustic electric shocks, burning flashes of liquid fire, whenever I tried to urinate. Marge insisted that I see a doctor immediately—IMMEDIATELY!— the quality of health care on Cod Cape at the time notwithstanding. (Marge had twisted her ankle jogging the year before and was diagnosed with gout.) My infidelity precluded putting it off, however. *Nolo contendere.* I was guilty.

The admissions clerk at the local clinic seemed to pick up on this—although at first I thought it was because I wasn't a local, in itself suspect—and greeted me with a cold silent stare.

"Hello." I smiled, but she wasn't having any of it. Everything about me looked like trouble. "I'm here to see a doctor. I have a kind of burning pain—"

"Speak up, please."

This was a delicate situation, one that begged privacy. Yet the closer in I moved the farther she backed away. "Well, I'm experiencing a burning—when I go to the bathroom."

"And where would that be?"

"On the second floor of the house."

"The burn wound," she said, deciding she was in dialog with an idiot. "Has it begun to blister?"

"I didn't say I have a burn wound, exactly, I said I have a burn*ing.*"

"Then where is the burn*ing,* exactly?"

There was no easy way to say this to a stranger, a woman, in a crowded reception room. I therefore tried to mouth the words.

"Speak up, please."

"You know, in my. . . ." I dropped my eyes to my groin.

"Sir, I can't hear you."

"IN MY PENIS. I HAVE A BURNING PAIN IN MY PENIS."

Every head in the room shot up. "You'd better come with me."

I was directed down a long yellow corridor where a nurse in square white shoes, white stockings, and a starched Florence Nightingale cap looked me up and down with her fists firmly anchored to her hips. Without a word she led me to an egg-shaped man wearing a stethoscope and perched on a creaky wooden chair with wheels.

"Well let me see it, let me see it." He waved at my trousers while pawing through a cluttered desk drawer. As I lowered my zipper the nurse glanced uneasily at the exit sign, unsure what exactly I was going to reveal, a bomb, a gun, a chancre-covered sack of pus. The doctor wheeled forward while untwisting a paperclip that he meticulously straightened to its full length, preparing to begin the examination.

"Open the *meatus*," he growled, barely parting his lips to speak. Mē-ā′təs. I had never heard the word. "The *meatus*, the *meatus*," he repeated, indicating the tip of my penis. I froze upon hearing the snap of the nurse's rubber gloves. Confused, and therefore paralyzed, I didn't know what they wanted, until the nurse pinched it open like the mouth of a baby bird. With the first jab of the paper clip I staggered into the doctor, whose chair rolled over the nurse's foot. Enough! The nurse tore off her gloves. I would have to seek help elsewhere.

"But where?" This was the only clinic within forty-five miles. "Where?" I followed her to the door.

"Elsewhere, elsewhere," she shouted, as if giving a deaf beggar directions to hell.

Marge, no stranger to casual sex, was angry and understandably wounded, but nonetheless making an effort to forgive me. In my absence, however, she, too, had begun to experience a burning sensation. We left immediately for Boston where she had scheduled an appointment with her gynecologist who referred me to a urologist, post-haste.

A well-fed, bull-necked fellow with an avuncular laugh and long silver-tipped cavalry mustaches, he dismissed the Cape doctor as a back-country moron and referred to himself as "the old army doc," as in "The old army doc has served the troops on four continents," and "There's nothing the old army doc hasn't seen." Indeed the examination room was decorated with color photographs of anal genital herpes and pubic lice. Cheerfully describing the various shades and textures of discharge—milky, cottage cheesy, green—he began his examination. "So you had a sexual encounter outside marriage?"

"Well, my partner and I aren't married."

"The old one-night stand." His chuckle held a hint of nostalgia.

"Two," I corrected him. "One-night stands."

"Besides the partner?" His eyebrows peaked. With a waiting room full of swollen prostates, his morning was suddenly getting interesting. "Not allergic to penicillin are you?"

"Will that cure it?"

"If you have syphilis it will."

"I might have syphilis?"

"Any lesions or chancres?"

"No."

"Any pustulating sores? Gumma on your anus? Your face?"

"Gumma?"

"Round tumorous masses. I treated an old man in Korea whose face looked like a sack of golf balls. No coloration on your shorts?"

"I haven't noticed any."

"Oh, you'd notice. Bunch of my boys in Pusan, half the damn platoon, came down with the clap. Their shorts were the color of eggs over easy." He handed me a glass slide and instructed me to hold it in front of my penis while he opened a fresh tube of surgical jelly. "Hold tight to the table now."

"But I haven't had any discharge."

"Not to worry, the old army doc can get blood from a stone. Ready?" he asked, and pressed my prostate like a doorbell until one tiny droplet dribbled onto the slide. Later that evening he telephoned with the results. "Chlamydia!" he proclaimed with the enthusiasm of a proud grandpa announcing the name of a newborn.

3.

Many men would have to admit that the sole reason they have even half a chance with a woman who is in all measurable ways more intelligent and financially independent, socially astute and imbued with a firm sense of life purpose, is that they are some kind of improvement over the previous guy; a WIFP, as the expression goes, a Work in F**king Progress. I was not as a rule unfaithful. Yes, there had been Wendy. But Marge was married and living with another man at the time. And yes again, the one anomalous weekend. But I was not some kind of man ho. I did not hit on Marge's friends. Or try to impress these friends of Marge's with four-star restaurant meals billed to the family credit card. I did not install my girlfriends in the guest room or sing lugubrious Appalachian folk songs on the auto harp when one of them dumped me. Yes, I had given Marge an STD. But I was not her ex-husband.

Marge was a reformed roué, a woman of admitted sexual experience and curiosity. I didn't expect her to pump her fists and shout, Hey, I might have pelvic inflammatory disease but it beats living with a man who doesn't want to share my bed. I didn't expect her to choke down 500 mg of erythromycin four times a day and shrug, Who cares about nausea, stomach pain, and vomiting, Woody's got my back. But the fact is, I did. I wasn't jealous of the attention she received. I was more than happy to take up the slack at home when she was on the road and honored to be asked to read the early drafts of her fiction and offer feedback. All of which the ex considered to be a drag.

I was ashamed of myself. I was ready, begging by now,

to commit to monogamy. Her husband had never been. Even when I knew she was angry and feeling vulnerable, wondering if she would ever be able to trust me again, our strengths and weaknesses were oddly counterbalanced. Marge was good at making money but never able to save it. I was my father's son, cheap. She didn't have a retirement plan. I'd studied the market but had never had a dime to invest.

Some days before Thanksgiving, Marge received a cryptic summons from her mother in Florida. Come down here, her mother demanded. As soon as possible, she insisted. I have something to give you. And most mysteriously: Take the car.

In poems and novels, Marge's mother emerged as an impoverished and embittered working class housewife from inner city Detroit, and more, an insidious manipulator. She was a psychic, according to Marge, able to perceive the innermost secrets of strangers and read the palms of neighbor women who lined up outside her kitchen door for the privilege. She was resentful of having had to quit high school in the tenth grade to work as a chambermaid and, jealous of her daughter's opportunities, she had tried to prevent Marge from taking a scholarship to one of the best universities in the country so she might remain living at home and pay rent. She was prone to fits of childish petulance. In one family story, upset with her husband's late arrival for dinner, she dumped a stew she'd been cooking for hours into the garbage can. Powerless, however, in the face of her husband's violent temper—he once slammed the car door on Marge's hand because she was slow to climb into the back seat—Marge's mother attempted to wield absolute control over her daughter, sniffing her underpants for evidence of sexual activity, finding and reading her hidden diaries, subjecting her boyfriends, and later in life Marge's husband, to unyielding ridicule. In fact her ex-husband flat out refused to visit his in-laws ever again.

"What exactly does your mother want to give you?" I asked.

Marge couldn't even guess.

"Why the hurry?"

"She said it had to be before Christmas."

"But your mother is Jewish."

Many things about her mother were a complete mystery to Marge.

"Why do you have to drive twelve-hundred miles?"

"I assume it's too big to take back on the plane."

"What is?"

"She wouldn't say."

What I was about to experience upon meeting her mother was inexplicable and is to this day, bizarre, as close as I have ever come to encountering the supernatural. I had no way of knowing any of this at the time, only that Marge and I were partners and friends as much as we were lovers, however long we might remain together. I knew that visits with her mother were emotionally wrenching for Marge. I gathered, too, that this visit might be the last and I wasn't about to ask her to face it alone.

4.

I had seen photographs of Marge's mother and I was expecting an intimidating matriarch with Marge's dark penetrating eyes and loose black hair, but it was a white-haired lady, slender and frail, who opened the door of their small retirement home in Tequesta. She was perhaps four-and-a-half feet tall with a coquettish gleam in her eyes and a soft hopeful smile. She led us to the kitchen table and an old aluminum pot full of something lumpy and thick with a brown gelatinous gravy reminiscent of motor oil. "It's lamb stew," she whispered. "But I have to say it's beef or *he* won't eat it."

He? I looked around. "I'm not really hungry," I said.

She nodded with quiet understanding, "You still worry about your weight."

How did she know that? "I'm not worried about my weight."

"People make life miserable for overweight children."

I turned silently to Marge. Obesity was the shame of my childhood. You told her that?

Marge slowly shook her head, of course not.

Then how did she...?

Marge shrugged, She just *knows*.

Her mother patted the chair next to hers at the kitchen table. "Have some," she said. It was not a question.

He, who I realized was always Marge's father, was enveloped in an enormous Naugahyde recliner watching TV. No longer the sadistic despot who once gave his wife a gift-wrapped mop for her birthday, he was a pallid old man with smudged eye-glasses, a half-zipped fly and the bewildered expression of someone stranded on an island between two lanes of traffic. He was happy enough to have visitors but confused as this was Tuesday and the visiting nurse came on Wednesdays. Nonetheless he rolled up his sleeve to have his blood pressure checked and chuckled, "Heh, heh, heh," the only sounds I heard from him as long as the visit lasted.

Marge's mother entered the living room with a thick folder of newspaper clippings. She took a seat next to me on the couch and placed them one after another on my lap. Some were yellow and crumbling, decades old.

"Mother likes to talk about current events," Marge said by way of explanation.

"I don't know," I responded politely after giving each one a glance. "I really haven't put much thought into President Carter's dealings with Anwar Sadat."

"He's no use at conversation." Her mother sniffed at her husband. "How about this?" She handed me an article about the introduction of a mechanical heart called the Jarvic-7.

"Don't know much about medicine, I'm afraid."

"You were in the slow reader group in grade school, weren't you?"

I had never told that to anyone. Not Marge. Not one soul.

Marge looked at the ceiling.

At four-ten it was time for dinner and they were taking

us to the best restaurant in town. The parking lot of Bob's Muddy Rudder was mobbed to overflow. Pushing through the early-bird crowd to the hostess stand, Marge's mother announced our arrival and was told to wait in the lounge, a dark, low-ceilinged room throbbing with reggae, lit only by fish tanks. "But we have reservations," her mother insisted. Then she turned to her husband. "Did you make the reservations?"

"Heh, heh, heh."

"Mother, we could try another restaurant," Marge suggested.

Crestfallen, she looked longingly at the potted palm trees on the outdoor deck and the view of the natural gas facility across the canal. "But I've always wanted to eat here."

"How long?" I asked the hostess, who sized up the importance of Marge's parents. She was perfectly polite, running her fingers through the names in her reservation book, but I'd worked in the restaurant trade and her body language was clear enough: Why don't you nice folks go and try the Taco Bell on South Dixie Highway?

Marge's mother was near tears. "What did she say?"

"That they're booked solid."

"You don't get along with your mother, do you?" she said.

We found a steak house in a nearby strip mall. The décor was tired, the crowd ancient, the waitresses overworked. "They have chicken, they have seafood. Look, Dad, ribs!" Marge, apparently sensing trouble, did her best to settle us in for a pleasant meal. "It's a nice big menu, Mother, isn't it?"

In fact her mother had completely disappeared behind it, muttering a string of epithets. "It's shit, all shit," her mother hissed. "A stinking shit menu."

Marge ordered a bottle of wine.

"What would you like, Mother? Fresh tuna? They have very nice shrimp. Red grouper. And Mahi Mahi. . . ."

"Piss. Shit and molasses."

Marge ordered broiled tuna for her mother, ribs for her dad, but no sooner had the waitress delivered the main courses than her mother's entree had disappeared, the plate empty except for a small serving of julienned carrots. "This is puke. Not eating puke," Marge's mother muttered, folding a half-pound tuna steak in an oil-stained linen napkin and stuffing it into her purse. "I'm bringing it home to the cat."

"Can I pour you another glass of wine?" I asked.

"Please," Marge said.

"You drink too much." Her mother fixed me with a cold stare. "And you better stop it with those drugs."

I smiled weakly, as if to slough off a bad joke, but inside I was ice. Could she know about the cocaine, this little woman who lived twelve-hundred miles away? Marge didn't know about the cocaine. I believed it now. She was a mind reader, just as Marge had said. She was some kind of savant or a mutant out of the X-Men comics. I understood why Marge was overly secretive at times, why she got angry if she ever came upon me searching for something, even a pencil, in her desk drawers, why she clammed up if I came near when she was on the telephone. It was pure self-defense.

A moment before, I had had the illusion of something flying past my eyes. An insect, I'd surmised, but just now something hit me in the neck. When I saw the waitress bring her hand to her ear, I realized it was Marge's mother. She was rolling tiny balls of rye bread and throwing them while her litany of curses got louder. "Fuck. Balls. Shit and molasses."

"Mother, please, stop it." Marge grabbed the breadbasket. "Mother what are you doing? Dad, what is she doing?"

"Heh, heh, heh."

When we arrived at their house the following morning, Marge's mother was vibrant, wearing a black and white checkered dress and red lipstick, cheeks flushed with mischief. "He's not here." She seemed years younger, giddy with relief. "He's playing pinochle." She steered us to the couch. "He won't be back till eleven."

As Marge and I sat in wait, her mother darted from room to room. Drawers flew open, boxes tumbled from closets, shoes were scattered, the freezer door slammed. Returning again and again to the couch she dropped wads of dollar bills in our laps. They were rolled tightly, crumpled, folded, bound with rubber bands. The pile grew too large for us to hold and toppled to the floor.

But she kept returning, out of breath, digging treasure out of sewing boxes, flower vases, old boots, jelly jars, the backs of stuffed chairs, anywhere she could hide it from her husband, years upon decades of one-dollar bills secretly hoarded and hidden out of sight.

"This is what she wanted to give us?" I asked Marge. We looked at the pile, maybe a thousand dollars in all. "But why did we have to drive down?"

"Come help me with this," her mother called. We found her rooting through the back of a closet, pushing aside a card table, old rubber boots, winter coats they hadn't worn since they'd left Detroit. Upon locating an enormous cardboard box she had me haul it onto the bed. Dust blew up in a plume. The box flaps crumbled. "Careful!" She sounded afraid. "Please be careful." As I prepared to dig out the contents she edged me aside, plunged her hands in the box and proceeded to remove Christmas ornaments wrapped in yellowed tissue paper, carousel horses, golden bells, rhinestone-studded eggs— all decades old, all purchased from dime-stores—sleighs, angels blown from glass, candy canes, ballerinas, a winking Cheshire cat.

"I collected them," she whispered. "Every one." Raised in an orthodox Jewish family and having married a Presbyterian, this was tantamount to sin. "It's all yours now." She beamed at Marge and me. Here was her treasure to bequeath: too fragile to take on a plane and along with the mound of dollar bills too large for a suitcase; only a car was sufficient to carry it all away.

When the morning came to say our good-byes, I strolled to the curb with Marge's father. He had liked having another man around and had warmed to my presence even as he still seemed somewhat puzzled as to who I was. "Well, thank you for a terrific visit," I said, pumping his thin and weightless hand.

But her mother had something more to say, something private, and I watched them as they tarried on the front steps, Marge trying to get away as she must have tried all her life and her mother clinging to her elbow, refusing to let go.

"I want to see you marry him," her mother said. This from a true psychic, from a woman who had read me inside out, who had never met me before and never would again, but somehow knew my past, my character, my every rotten indiscretion. And still she insisted, "Marry him."

"Mother, I've been married twice."

"So what? So have I."

"This is ridiculous. I just got divorced."

"Are you listening to me?"

"Do you know how much younger he is?"

All of this was repeated to me, of course. I could make out very little at the time. I could see Marge trying to avoid her mother's eyes and then submitting to a stronger will, looking deeply into them with the same skeptical skew of her lips that must have punctuated decades of mother daughter disagreements. What passed between them was as inexplicable to me as the bond between a mother with a tenth-grade education and a daughter who was to write forty-five books, as improbable as a middle child in an immigrant family of nine children instructing her own daughter how to perform an abortion on herself and the terrified college freshman who had the strength to do it.

"I know he's a good man," her mother insisted.

"Enough." Marge kissed her mother's cheek. "Good bye. I'll call you."

"Marry him," were the last words her mother was to say to Marge in person.

And in spite of everything Marge knew about me, and everything she was about to discover, she did.

THE SYLLOGISM

A syllogism, you may recall from Logic 101, is an argument containing three propositions, two of which are premises and the third a conclusion, to wit: Drugs make you stupid. You do drugs all the time. Therefore, you are too stupid to know how stupid you are. I grasped this in my sophomore year of college, not in the classroom but on the day I sought out the secret address of a place to buy acid. Passed on to me in a whisper, the place was impossible to miss. Indeed, if I happened upon a complete stranger to the neighborhood and asked, "Where can I buy LSD?" he would probably shrug, "How am I supposed to know? Try that dump with the purple door."

The purple door was never locked. If this didn't strike you as stupid enough, in lieu of a curtain in the front bay window there was a big red flag with a stencil cut of a marijuana plant. Entering for the first time I was blown back with the odor of cat urine so strong my eyes swelled shut. The front room was dark, lit only by a bare blue light bulb swinging on a wire. A naked man, hairy and thin, stood in the middle of the floor on a mat of outspread newspapers. He was surrounded by an admiring circle of young women wearing long beaded earrings and gauze-thin halter tops. He turned in slow circles, arms pressed to his sides like the wings of a trussed turkey, and smiled beatifically as the women cooed encouragement. "Let it go," their soft voices whispered. "Let it all go and be free."

Cast in blue light his shriveled cock and balls were like robin eggs in a wire nest. His tongue flicked at his coarse black beard. "Let it go," the chanting went on. Over and over the soft voices chanted, "Let it go, be free. . . ." The man squeezed his eyes in fierce concentration. One woman exhorted him, "There is no past. There is only now. Be here now. . . ," she rocked forward and back as if in a trance, ". . . and be free."

I couldn't see it from where I stood, but heard it hit the newspapers, like the smack of two cupped palms. The odor crossed the room as chanting gave way to applause. He raised his arms in victory each time he squeezed out another turd and shouted "Freedom! Freedom!" while turning in box steps on the sticky newspaper.

At the time I was smoking a lot of marijuana. I was paranoid about everything, perennially tired, late with my class work, depressed, anxious, and forgetful. One day at breakfast, my first joint of the day in one hand, a coffee cup in the other, I was complaining to a roommate about the sorry state of my inexplicably miserable life. She said, "Maybe you should stop smoking dope." This struck me as a revelation. In all the times I had pondered my problems, all the while smoking dope, I had never come to this conclusion. Remember the syllogism.

But there was one drug that seemed to make you smart. Cocaine made you smart. Cocaine was the opposite of marijuana. It sharpened the intellect and shattered the inner censor. Even better, cocaine felt like something I'd been waiting for all my life.

When I was a child I was clumsy and overweight, something of a laughing stock in school, and an embarrassment to my parents who felt, certainly with my best interests at heart, that I would have a much better chance in life if I became thin and wiry, an athletic American boy. The prevailing treatment at the time, routinely prescribed by pediatricians, was dextroamphetamine, administered in enormous black capsules. Commonly issued to combat troops and popular with cross-country truck drivers, these were known on the street as Black Beauties. The *Urban Dictionary* describes the effects as "a mild to moderate euphoria, increased hyperactivity, increased awareness of surroundings, increased interest in repetitive or normally boring activities, decreased appetite, and decreased ability to sleep," which just about nails the way I went through elementary school. When I got older and read the beat poets I discovered that speed was commonly used by hipsters in an era of stifling conformity, the experience enhanced by cigarettes, espresso, jazz, and intense conversation. But I was ten years old. I had grandma, Hebrew school, and years of inexplicably sleepless nights filled with nothing but doo-wop and Jean Shepherd on the all-night radio. I have no idea of the medical repercussions of a childhood hooked on diet pills, only that I experienced life as a treadmill set at high, going nowhere very fast. I wondered why my friends didn't spend entire afternoons rereading the same paragraph in the World Book Encyclopedia, or watching in euphoric wonderment as an ant climbed the window jamb. Which is why, when I did coke for the first time, I experienced a fuzzy and romantic longing for the past. My childhood came back to me: the shakes, the grinding teeth, the dry mouth, and above all the sublime ability to focus, to shut out everything in this vast and complicated world except repetitive or normally boring activities. Like writing.

Coke gave you not only the concentrative facility to immerse yourself in any insignificant task whatsoever, but the conviction that whatever arse-backwards and pointless thing you were doing deserved the Nobel Prize. As a child I could make no use of this facility but now the adrenaline rush, the confidence, the exquisite ability to concentrate at last had a focus. I have read that Robert Louis Stevenson wrote *The Strange Case of Dr. Jeckyl and Mr. Hyde* in six days. For some time he had been musing on the idea of the duality of good and evil coexisting in a man's nature. But while sick in bed, taking a medication suffused with a potent cocaine derivative popular in Victorian times, he wrote the first draft in a kind of frenzy, running down the stairs in his bathrobe, reading drafts to Ms. Stevenson, tearing back upstairs with her encouragement to write more. If I can extrapolate from my own experience it was the confluence of idea and drug that enabled him to write so quickly. I seriously doubt it was just the cocaine. If it was the drug alone he would have run downstairs to beg Ms. Stevenson for a quickie and run back up to write nothing but drivel. Or so it went with me and Ms. Piercy.

I was turned on for the first time at a dinner party and remember stealing into the bathroom to take notes on a roll of toilet paper. For months I'd been grinding away on a second novel that was supposed to be funny, and here I had discovered the perfect tool to complete it. At 4 A.M. every day I drank a huge mug of coffee and chopped my first lines of coke. Within seconds I was overtaken by voice. It wrung my nerves and flowed through my fingers. It was the voice of my loud and sarcastic Brooklyn uncles, of comedians in Catskill mountain hotels, the New York Jewish voice that excited and nurtured me as a child but began to fade when I went to college then moved to New England, as I tried ever harder to fit in and tone it down. I finished the first draft of the novel in a matter of months only to begin the long frustrating process of submitting it for publication. And that's when the problem started.

I was finished with the novel but not the coke. I was like a runaway subway train speeding underground with no passengers. I had the energy, I had the concentration, I had the time, but there was more milk in a green coconut than ideas in my head. I was a hyper-graphic perpetual motion machine overwhelmed with the urge to write. Regardless of the quality or the content, I wrote pages and pages and with no inclination to revise. I had a stack of yellow legal pads a foot thick, every page covered front to back in illegible longhand scrawl. And because I was on cocaine and totally empowered, completely without fear, I thought every word profound.

As I was now living with Marge, over a hundred miles from Boston, I procured my drugs on Cape Cod, from a middle-aged iron woman who surfed, swam long distances outdoors seven months a year and ran a furniture restoration business on her own. She lived in an old farm house near Pleasant Bay with an enormous yellow barn, did her deliveries in a two-ton pickup truck, boasted a string of lovers that included the most famous abstract expressionists in the New York school, and cared for an ever increasing pride of cats fathered by a huge calico tom named Caesar. Although her skin was as tough as a lizard's, wrinkled by age and weather, she cut a handsome figure, with a tight athletic body, high cheek bones, a Maori tattoo on her bicep, silver white hair which she grew to her waist, and heavy native jewelry made of ivory and turquoise. Raised in New Zealand, she'd been an Olympic swimmer before locating to Manhattan where she operated an antique gallery on Lexington Avenue. In the late seventies she moved to Cape Cod with her much older husband, an architect who succumbed to cirrhosis of the liver. Since his death she'd had a series of affairs with much younger and very buff seasonal workers from Jamaica who became her source of drugs.

Although she hosted dinner parties for gallery owners and antique dealers and their wives—smoky, vodka-swelled affairs in which the drinking began at eight and it wasn't until ten-thirty that she absently strolled into the kitchen to start the roast—she was a woman who mostly liked men, who identified with men, with the image of the archetypal tough guys and outlaws of her generation. Because I was a man who had come of age in an era of less extreme sexual identities and found her attitudes as naïve as they were outdated, we treated each other with caution.

She was fun company in a group but tête-à-tête conversation was difficult with a woman who referred to her last one-night-stand as a henpecked wuss for returning to his wife, or a temperamental woman friend as deserving a good hard bitch slap. However, she was the only person I knew who always had quality cocaine. No hundred-mile trips to Boston, and worse, the long slow paranoid drives home, eyes scouring the rear-view for a state trooper; no loud sports bars enduring a TV hockey game while waiting for a white suburban college drop-out dealer who fancied himself a gangsta. I could shop safely, on-Cape, except for one glitch. My dealer was perfectly happy to receive a kilo of coke flown up from Kingston inside a gift box of mangoes, cut it into tightly wrapped origami-like one-gram packages and sell them at an enormous profit, but she saw herself as a craftsperson, an athlete, a doyenne of the furniture restoration business, and did not like to think of herself as selling drugs.

Therefore every desperate attempt on my part to score and likewise every opportunity on hers to move product occasioned the semblance of a formal social visit.

Although I never called her unless I wanted drugs, and as my habit grew had to do so on a regular basis, she received each phone call with an eruption of surprise, as if I had unexpectedly turned up after a three-year backpacking adventure in the Hindu Kush. "Oh, look who's here. Your old lady let you out of the house without your leash?"

"Just in the neighborhood."

"Oh, yeah?" As she lived about forty miles away this was a lie too ridiculous to acknowledge. "What's new?"

Under the best of circumstances this question has the potential to immobilize me in a state of profound introspection. Nothing is ever really new with me. The alarm rings at seven. I make café au lait. I work out on a rowing machine while watching ESPN SportsCenter. I spend the better part of every day with my face in a MacBook Pro, writing something that at best no one will see for years. On St. Patrick's Day I plant the peas; on Thanksgiving morning I spread manure. Even something out of the ordinary, a vacation, a gall bladder operation, a large check in the mail, has been anticipated for some time so it does not meet the criteria of new. Add to this state of bewilderment the fact that I have been watching my stash diminish, putting off calling her until I am totally desperate for drugs, sitting in my car within sight of her front door at eight-thirty in the morning. "Uh, not much new with me. You?"

Unfortunately everything. "Hey, Caesar got another little bitch pregnant, did I tell you that?" Last month. "That stud has the biggest balls I've ever seen on a cat. You ever see his balls?" She had pointed them out on numerous occasions. "You know what he left me?"

"A dead squirrel on your door mat."

"I told you that? More than my limp-dick ex-boy-friend ever did for me. You know the new antenna he put on the pickup? It fell off. He was a worse mechanic than he was a fuck. . . ." There was more. Her bidet was leaking. A seagull had dropped a quahog that dented her windshield. Her favorite female cat had fleas. It is frankly unfathomable to me that someone would consider the minor irritations of daily life to be of even remote conversational interest but it was as if I had turned a spigot that came off in my hand. She didn't have enough avocados to make guacamole. She craved Chimichangas but they gave her gas.

As usual I awaited any chance to seize an opening. "So, you'll be home? I could pick up some avocados in town."

Once inside her house there were the cats to admire, as well as any new pieces of furniture she had restored, music she was currently listening to. Tea was served. There were stories about people I had never met, an armoire the size of a refrigerator freezer to be lifted from her truck, at which point I'd ask, as absently as I could, "You have any coke?"

She never answered the question directly but shrugged resignedly and ascended the stairs to her bedroom, leaving me no choice but to follow. "You and Marge still fuckin'?" she'd ask, rummaging through her night table drawer. "A lot of guys stop fucking their wives." But as I stood at the foot of her king bed, a cat on my shoulder, a mug of cold chai in my hand, trying not to look at the erotic painting over her bed or the enormous silicone dildo or the oozing tube of KY jelly and above all her breasts, falling out of her open bathrobe, a headache coming on, my morning shot to shit, all I wanted was to overpay for a few grams of cocaine and get out of there.

"My husband used to fuck me every day of the week. I ever tell you that?" Indeed she had. "That man had a cock like an Indian elephant."

And so it went every time, usually for an hour or more, until she, too, grew bored, or decided I was some kind of neutered asexual half-man for not making a pass, or an interior alarm went off signaling the requisite amount of time had gone by to designate this a visit and not a drug deal. Then, "Hey!" she would say, as if just remembering, as if she had eight starving people over for dinner and had yet to put the roast in the oven. "I got some really good shit," she would say, and sell me my drugs so I could go home.

My wife is a writer of prodigious literary output but some day it will be discovered by an astute grad student connecting the dots in her archive that her production increased significantly on the day that I rented an office outside the house. Working with someone like me under the same roof is a challenge even for those with unshakable concentration, impossible if you are at all sensitive to the sounds of a creature in pain. When one is told that he snores, it is difficult to believe. It is tempting to say, Prove it, tape me. But no one ever does. Once, at the end of a short call, I accidentally left my phone off the hook with the answering machine running and discovered that listening to myself writing is like being in bed next to someone with obstructive sleep apnea. Even people in my office building will occasionally ask after me, having heard me through the walls groaning or talking to myself or come upon me wandering the parking lot in a cold sweat. In the years that I was doing cocaine, however, I was working at home. I was quietly engaged in my study for hours, as my wife was in hers. She had no idea what was going on. I had always been prone to peaks of euphoria that alternated with troughs of intense envy and pessimism. I had always had a frantic drive for sex. Moreover, I tended not to show the effects of coke wearing off until the cocktail hour. For someone who had no idea that her husband had developed a secret drug habit

I must have seemed an awful lot like a frustrated writer who drank. Except for the money. The money kept disappearing.

In the beginning I was spending about a hundred dollars a week on coke, not much more than a weekly restaurant tab or chain-smoking habit; an amount I could reasonably extract from my checking account. But coke made writing feel so good, so effortless, that I began to snort a bit for other unpleasant activities, like cleaning the bathroom, like figuring the taxes, like doing anything that was a pain in the ass to do. One hundred a week was suddenly three hundred a week and my personal savings were suddenly gone.

I found a freelance job writing software content for a toy company that had made its mark selling leather hobby kits and plastic backyard pools, and some decades later a doll so wildly popular that at Christmas there were shortages causing parents to fight it out in the toy store aisles to get one. The heirs of the company then went hi-tech and developed what might have been the world's slowest personal computer. I was called upon to write amusing content for educational word games and was paid to come up with funny word searches, quizzes and acrostics. I wasn't writing literature but who cared? I was on coke! I was harnessed to a project, making good money. I was part of the silicon revolution, a tech writer with a well-known company and best of all allowed to work at home. Most days I wrote from early morning till late afternoon happily surrounded by a dictionary, a thesaurus, encyclopedias, children's books, and legal pads, stacks of legal pads densely filled with puzzles and puns, until about four, when my eyes began to burn and my heart raced, when my hands shook and my temples ached, when the euphoria turned into anxiety and I had a secret to face. The money I was making simply did not exist. After eight months I had spent every dime I'd made on coke.

I was as low as I had ever been in my life and pondering any number of desperate measures. Once, years before, at the encouragement of a friend who convinced me that a third glass of wine at dinner was a warning sign for the early onset of alcoholism, I attended a 12 step program and discovered a bizarre universe in which the people with the most messed up lives had the most status. While I sat in the back row, unacknowledged and alone, the guy who backed over his dog with a station wagon got a round of applause. The mother-of-three who became a prostitute had so many offers from men volunteering to be her sponsor that she took names and numbers on a napkin. It felt like a talent show for addicts. I thought I might return now that I had become as desperate as the other contestants but I convinced myself that I had my wife's reputation to protect. She was a famous writer. I had already deceived her and drained my savings. What would be the consequences if I went public with my need for help, if people discovered she was married to a coke addict? We lived in a small town where your secrets are only as safe as where you're parked:

anywhere you go, anything you do, people are aware of it because they see your car. Proving the perfect logic of the syllogism once again, I took another long snort of cocaine and reasoned that I could not seek help because I needed to protect the person I was hurting most and therein stumbled upon the greatest rationalization known to man: blame the victim.

This was a finding of far-reaching personal import, rivaling such formative developmental breakthroughs as discovering that playing with your genitals makes you feel really good, or that mixing mayonnaise and ketchup makes Russian dressing. Armed with this discovery, I could blame my wife for getting hooked on cocaine in the first place. Didn't I want to write a great novel that would earn us lots of money? Didn't I want her to stop working so hard and traveling so much to support us? Blaming the victim had real possibilities. Everything could be her fault. I suddenly had a worldview. It all made sense. I wasn't personally responsible for anything. Nothing was my fault. For instance, there was a reason I wasn't successful. Study after study showed that tall men had more reproductive success, made more in the marketplace, got promoted faster. But I am only five-feet-eight inches tall. And whose fault was that? My mother's, of course! Why didn't she marry a taller guy? The bitch! I had always been delusional but coke took it to another level.

One night, however, the unthinkable happened. One night everything changed. It began as casually as any ordinary night. After a day of snorting coke and fruit-lessly scribbling in my legal pad, I induced the requisite charm to convince my wife to go to bed with me. But as we began to kiss, as we left articles of clothing on pieces of furniture and made our way to bed, as we lay face to face, I realized that something horrible was happening: actually, not happening. With the awesome power of a spiritual conversion I understood the implications of taking this drug: the implications to my body, to my circulatory system, to my marriage, to my future. For the first time in my life, I could not get it up. I had coke dick, and, with the insight available to the catastrophic imagination jacked to a flaming paranoid frenzy, I had a vision of my future.

I would never make love again. I would be a useless husband. I would be asked to leave. I would wander the streets a toothless, homeless vagabond, sleeping on sub-way grates, dying an unclaimed corpse under a highway bridge.

At that moment, I looked deep into the eyes of my partner, who was stifling a yawn and checking the clock radio over my shoulder and asking me if I didn't want to maybe try again later when I felt more like making love because she actually had things to do, and I understood that if I couldn't control this addiction, couldn't get a grip on my life, that my wife's life, too, would be ruined. Would she ever again find love? Would she become bit-ter? Would she suffer the mockery of friends? Would she fill the house with stray cats in lieu of real emotional connection, start padding around in slippers and babbling as lonely people do, unable to continue her work, to fulfill her life's mission?

Was it really possible that coke could make you impotent? I made a pledge at that moment to give up cocaine. Cold turkey. Forever.

And I did it, for her.

THE ONE WHO DIES
WITH THE MOST SEX WINS

Every traveler has a ritual. I once knew a painter who worked as a visiting artist to support herself. Half the year she was on the road, put up by various colleges in grad student high-rise housing or bleak off-campus motels. She told me she never felt comfortable in new spaces until she rendered them in paint, and immediately upon arrival set up her easel to capture the afternoon shadow on a garish polyester bed spread or the dolor of an empty closet with three wire hangers. A musician friend travels with a bottle of bourbon and drinks away his homesickness. My wife unpacks her suitcase and fills the drawers, for a one-night or five-night stay. I never felt comfortable in a strange place until I had sex.

We'd been offered the use of a fabulous house just outside Boston from Wednesday through the weekend. They kept a spare key above the lintel of the kitchen door. The owner was a friend of many years whom we'd known from the beginning of his skyrocketing career, from unknown literary novelist to Hollywood screenwriter and *New York Times* bestseller. In fact, he had said, he and his family would be leaving early Wednesday morning for a meeting in New York with the director of his next feature film. Three times the size of our own house on the Cape, it was one of those ornate Victorians in the Queen Anne style built for a family of ten, with projecting bay windows, a wrap-around porch, two round turrets, and a balcony with a view of the city skyline.

It was a warm and humid afternoon infused with that buttery yellow light characteristic of early September in New England, our first day back in the city since late May. The master bedroom had arched Palladian windows dappled by a cluster of lush Norway Maples and a freestanding antique mirror that could easily be tilted for a view of the bed. Why wait till tonight, why not make love right now? It seemed to me the right thing to do, as simple and impulsive an act as chasing a ball into the street or grabbing the handle of a sizzling fry pan.

My wife preferred love late in the day, after work; evening was usually best. For me it was always the earlier the better. In fact I like sex best in the morning, so we usually compromised, any time after noon. Indeed I thought about sex until we had it and until then my mind was clear for little else. For me there was a kind of anxiety attached: if we hadn't yet had sex how would I know that we'd ever have it again? No day was complete until we did. I could not think straight until we did. My body seemed to itch from the inside out and my writing, or I should say those hours consigned to writing, were suffused with a kind of wild and promiscuous imagery I was unable to harness on the page.

It was nothing we would not have done at home. We put fresh sheets on the bed, we washed and burrowed under the covers. I brought my face to my wife's warm magnificent breasts. She lifted my mouth to hers and it went fairly predictably after that. I believe I was beneath her, murmuring something endearing like "Oh, god I love this pussy!" when I saw the little boy at the door. He was wearing a Boston Red Sox baseball cap and holding a large plastic action toy. "Mommy," he said. "There are people in your bed and they're neked."

"Naked," she said, correcting him, and after steering him into the hall, strode up to the bed. "What the hell are you doing here?"

This was totally unfair. "You were leaving this morning for New York. Your husband told me. He said we could have the house."

"He said Thursday!"

"He said Wednesday!" And if she had had the decency to turn her back I would have retrieved my date book to prove it. No matter. They didn't speak to us again for eleven years.

In a *Village Voice* article on male body builders, I read about the side effects of taking HCG and Clomid, female fertility drugs, to enhance muscular development. According to a former Mr. Universe, before his testicles shriveled to walnuts and he grew sizeable breasts, he was driven by insatiable sexual need. He had five girlfriends and one night he drove the entire length of Long Island in a preter-human frenzy to fuck every one. Likewise a one-time Mr. America on tour was so horny he used to bang soda machines, lifting them in a bear hug and stuffing his junk inside the coin return slot. I had never taken a hormone pill in my life but I lived with a similar sexual urgency. Relationships with most women my own age were wired for disappointment. Until I met my wife I had yet to find someone whose sexual desire, or at least her willingness, had peaked at the same time as my own.

Maybe sex proved my worst fears false: I was not too hideous a creature to love. Or maybe fucking was just an ego rush, who knows? But sex was my singular accomplishment, my one positive definition of myself. If my friends were better educated, or had more books to their credit; if they were as buff as Greek warriors or born to privilege, at least I had sex every day. Sex was the calculus by which I measured my worth. Orgasm was a given, my partner's and my own. But the real test was numbers. Six days out of seven was satisfactory. Five days, tolerable. For years I kept abreast of national statistics to make sure I stayed well above the national mean.

We'd arrived at their summer cottage late in the afternoon. The location was a well kept secret from her fans; the directions near impossible to follow: somewhere halfway up a cliff overlooking the Atlantic. She was one of America's favorite short story writers, of an older generation, an eminence among literary figures. Although I had brought along a galley of my new book—a comment from her would be invaluable—it was a coup simply to have been invited. Even an overnight visit secured you a moment in literary history, the kind you see in black and white photographs in the biographies of legendary writers.

She and her husband showed us to our room, a back porch, actually, with large screen panels overlooking the white pine forest. They told us we'd have to excuse them, at their age they were used to a nap at this time of day. They'd see us in a few hours, at dinner. As the shadows gathered, the mosquitoes followed suit. A walk in the woods or on the path leading down to the cove was impossible in Maine at this time of day. The rest of the house, we were given to believe, was off-limits until this evening. So we unpacked the car. We read. I had not forgotten the embarrassing situation with our friend in Boston, but really, what was to stop us? For all I knew our hosts were making love at this moment. How often had we excused ourselves, telling our guests we were taking a little "nap"? We discussed it. We weighed the pros and cons. I begged. We kissed tentatively, listening for voices. We scuttled beneath the sheets. We peeled off our clothing with caution. We barely uttered a word. We were ready for each other in moments. I moved easily inside my wife, pressing my face into the pillow to stifle all sound.

My wife heard it first and gasped, throwing me off, pulling the blanket up to cover herself. I turned to see the blur of a red plaid shirt brushing past the screen window. We dressed. We returned to our reading. We sat at opposite ends of the porch. Only when we heard voices in the house, running water, the radio, did we join them for drinks in the living room. Not a word was mentioned about it.

That night we were woken by a thrashing under the floorboards of the porch accompanied by high pitched chirps and growling, and finally full-throated squeals. Whatever was under there was at war. Unable to fall asleep until dawn, we woke up to a hot sun on the corrugated roof and the overpowering smell of rotten eggs. "Quite a racket last night," I said to the writer's husband as I entered the kitchen for breakfast. "I think you might have skunks."

"Yup. Stinks pretty bad." He was washing dishes and did not turn to face me. "I assumed it was you people." Never did get a blurb from his wife.

Maybe it was a purely chemical reaction, the dopamine rush, the squirt of pleasure-inducing chemicals into the reward system of the brain, the exquisite sense of well-being, the high. Attention activates it for actors. Power does it for politicians. Gambling, even for 80-year-olds wearing fanny-packs full of quarters who turn up in Atlantic City by the busload. A neuroscientist named Wolfram Schultz at Cambridge University performed an experiment on monkeys, held their heads in a vice and squirted apple juice in their mouths while scanning their brains. Every time they got the apple juice their dopamine neurons exploded in pyrotechnic displays of white-hot pleasure. But when he withheld the juice the monkeys freaked, became disoriented, made loud screeching cries for help, tore at their restraints, beat their fists in despair. I could relate. Without the promise of sex, I was a monkey with a jones for apple juice.

I could make the case that our society was a victim of the same compulsion. What sold cars, beer, clothing? Is pornography not a thirteen-billion-dollar industry? If the entire society was consumed with sex, and I was having more sex than anyone in my age group, did it not follow that I was the most successful person I knew?

I laughed at guys who drove hundred-fifty-thousand-dollar Mercedes. I viewed fitness fetishists as lumpy bags of rock. Mansions, advanced degrees, academic prizes, were as foolish a way to prove oneself as a trophy room full of rhinoceros heads. Were any of these outward signs of success connected to the life force itself? Of course not. It was obvious to me that the one who dies with the most sex wins.

But this was my contest, my rules, and it had to be the right sex, faithful sex, monogamous partner sex. That was the key. I wasn't competing with teen movie actors or porn stars or insecure jocks like Wilt Chamberlain whose boast that he had slept with 20,000 different women was so pitifully obvious that the very need for novelty put his virility in doubt. What did it prove? A sex offender in prison can masturbate twenty times a day. Who *couldn't* get off with a different partner every night?

She was a world famous memoirist, a flamboyant hostess who served champagne with the venison stew. The first flakes had begun stirring in mid-morning, hours before we arrived for lunch. As the meal lingered and daylight grew dim, we agreed to spend the night. It only made sense. The snow by now lay in drifts obscuring the barn door and the drive back to Cape Cod would take eight hours in the best of conditions. The one motel we had passed on the highway looked like the set of a chainsaw massacre film and the better hotels were booked with skiers. When my wife and I discussed our options, I assured her I had no intention of having sex tonight, not in this, not in anyone else's house ever again.

After a light dinner we gathered in front of the fire for desert. The conversation was good and we talked about living in old farmhouses, well drilling, eccentric neighbors, gardens, small town politics as they applied to Vermont versus Cape Cod, and the modest pleasures of country life in general for we were all four of us transplants from the city. She and her husband were generous people. I emerged from an impromptu tour of their root cellar with gifts, jars of bread and butter pickles and a six-pack of homemade beer. When the subject turned to bad backs, a problem common among serious gardeners,

Marge mentioned that I gave her a deep muscle massage every morning and the woman gave her husband a look so cold I turned away from the poor man. She then asked if I wouldn't show him what it was I did for Marge. Sure. I figured I'd give her a brief shoulder rub and be done with it. She spread a blanket in front of the fire and pulled her sweater off. "Is this a good position?" she asked, unhooking her bra.

Her husband sat squarely in his rocking chair, knuckles white, feet pasted to the floor, breathing imperceptibly and staring into space as his wife purred with more pleasure than I could possibly be giving her. "Ooh, there. . . . Oh, good, that's so good. Lower now," she said, as she tugged her pants to the small of her back. "Oh, right there."

About my mother's age, she was a serious farmer and a lifelong tennis player, in her younger years a professional, with a tight muscular back that tapered in a perfect V to the faint dimples in her buttocks. Her muscles fluttered like surface water pushed by wind as I ran my fingers up her spine. I had begun the massage in the same position I worked on my wife's back, straddling her buttocks, but arched up in a panic as I felt myself getting excited, a situation my hostess was aware of judging from her smile. End of massage.

You'd have to be a complete idiot to alienate two more friends, no less another important literary contact, by making the same mistake, and that only in order to do something you could do more comfortably, and in total privacy, the following day at home. Moreover the guestroom seemed to have walls made of cardboard. We could hear them run water, brush their teeth, pad in their slippers across the bedroom floor above us. I reached across the old bed to caress my wife and the bedsprings squealed like an angry metallic pig.

"You don't really want to make love *now*?" she said.

I was about to make my case when a voice, as if standing next to me said, "I think I'm going downstairs to get a glass of hot milk," but whoever said it was not in the room.

"Not a chance." My wife rolled away, and I lay awake for some hours listening to the wind rush up the ancient chimney, questioning this foolish attachment of mine. Why was I counting? Why did I put my wife through this embarrassment? What was I out to prove, to myself, to all those imaginary competitors totally unaware of my delusional scorecard?

How moronic to quantify sensuality, to measure self-worth by the numbers. Preoccupied with counting every sexual encounter, every odd place we made love and every new position, there was no room for living, for feeling, only competing. How ridiculous.

Back in those days I couldn't imagine being contented with a simple country life, with the satisfaction to be had from a long walk at dusk along the backshore beaches, say, or working in my garden, or serious reading, or even meditation. I'm glad to say that my preoccupation with sex is over. I'm on to more fulfilling things.

YOU'RE MARRIED TO HER?

Just in this past year I walked an average of thirty miles a week, grew eighty tomato plants with fruits as big as a pound each, read well over fifty books on my Kindle, and meditated twice a day for thirty minutes. You?

HAMMER AND FLAY

At one time or another all elected officials are asked how they got their start in public life. I believe I can trace my own political beginnings to the night my wife and I politely declined an invitation to have three-way sex with a hunchback.

Giancarlo Fossi was a local legend and in our small Cape Cod town, the object of almost boundless beneficence and affection, a sought-after dinner guest and an animated raconteur brimming with stories of rooming with Brando in Provincetown, living as an ex-pat in Paris after World War Two, and working for the National Lawyers' Guild, which was attacked during the McCarthy era as being a communist front. Years later I would learn that he was named in the Venona Papers as a Soviet spy, but at the time I simply hoped Jonny, as everyone called him, might become a friend.

Upon giving up my apartment and my restaurant job in Boston and moving full time to the Cape, I was basically starting all over again. For all the weekends I'd been visiting Marge I'd made no friends of my own and had little context in which to meet them. With no kids in the schools; no job in the fisheries, the building trades or even a real estate office; no boat, no desire to spend my mornings in a coffee shop or my nights in a bar; an unknown writer who spent all day alone at his desk, I rarely met a guy my age we didn't hire to repair something around the house. I didn't surf, farm shellfish, hunt, or belong to AA. Truth is, I just didn't seem to fit in, even on a short stint working construction. On my first day I was asked, "You catch any o' that run o' blues up the gut?"

"I don't even have a fishing rod," I admitted. "Was it a particularly good catch?"

"Did he say *particularly*?"

At lunch I subtly moved under a shade tree. It wasn't that I didn't want to sit in a mound of gravel and talk about the price of sheet rock but that as soon as I opened a Tupperware container instead of a wad of tin foil, I aroused suspicion. "The fuck is that red goop?"

"Just leftovers."

"Of road kill?"

"No, no, dinner last night. When the zucchini, tomatoes, and eggplant all ripen at the same time, Marge makes ratatouille." I had to be safe here, their wives and mothers all had gardens.

"Rat whut?"

There were others, to be sure, who did not fit the

mold: lanky preppies slumming for a year before grad school who straddled the beams of the cathedral ceilings like circus performers; nonplussed alcoholics who could frame a wall or fall off it with equal detachment; but they had an expertise that bought them acceptance. Back then I posed a problem for men in the building trades. Everyone on the Outer Cape grew up with an understanding of homosexuality. Provincetown, like San Francisco and Greenwich Village, was a Mecca for gays. But metrosexuals, guys who liked women *and* Bruno Magli slip-ons, were an as yet unidentified species on construction crews. Had they asked me to write ad copy for a spec house, or to prepare a pesto bruschetta that would feed the entire crew for lunch, I would have proven my worth. But the first time they saw me try to frame a window I elicited the kind of testosterone-fueled contempt that aroused the mountain men in *Deliverance* to sodomy.

Since most of my city friends had been in the antiwar movement, I figured I'd have luck finding the same on the Outer Cape, which for the better part of a century had been a magnet for lefties. They'd run the gamut of political affiliations: communists, anarchists, socialists, Trotskyites, pacifists; and all had found a haven in these remote summer colonies where everyone knew their politics but didn't care as long as they stuck it out through the winter.

At the time there was a large group of progressives who'd come of age during the Great Depression, raised their children in the radical enclaves of the Upper West

Side and the Hudson Valley and retired out here. In the Outer Cape off-season they met in study groups to learn Yiddish and read ancient Greek. They took on the local political boss, debating him at town meeting, mocking him in letters to the editor, and eventually brought him down. I enjoyed their erudite conversation, their urbane style, and dinner parties. Two bourbons could restart a forty-year-old argument about the Spanish Civil War. I called them our friends but it never really worked. My wife got sick in the presence of heavy cigarette smoking, which they viewed as a right guaranteed by the U.S. Constitution. Asking anyone not to smoke in her presence, in our house or theirs, was as troublesome as the mention of feminism, which caused men of that generation to leap on table tops, their eyeballs rolling counter clockwise and their ears burning bright blue while steam blew out their asses.

I was therefore surprised one Saturday morning to see Marge in front of the bank on Main Street engaged in conversation with Jonny, the unquestioned darling of that very group. With a trim gray beard, a leonine profile and imploring brown eyes, Jonny was a delicately handsome man who had been deformed by childhood polio and suffered a curvature of the spine that emerged from his back like an outcropping of granite. His legs were stick-thin and twisted, causing him to bend forward from the waist while walking, which he did with the aid of a cane. He was so short that to speak with him obliged one to hover above him to hear. Indeed he had his arm around Marge's shoulder, pulling her closer still. Jonny had already begun to hobble off when I reached them but Marge was clearly troubled. There was a proposed change in the zoning laws, he had told her, one designed to decrease the number of new homes being built in town by increasing the size of buildable lots. As she could afford it over the years, Marge had bought a number of small lots surrounding her home. According to the proposed change in the law, those lots would become unbuildable, and therefore worth much less.

She didn't know any more than that, she'd find out what she could, she told me. Jonny had invited us over for dinner that evening to talk about it.

He lived in a modernist-style cottage provided him for life by a wealthy socialist friend in one of the most splendid locations on all of Cape Cod: the lee side of a grassy dune that reared up like a great white mountain of sand between a freshwater kettle pond and Thoreau's Outer Beach. To get to Jonny's you drove cautiously over a single-lane sand road with steep sides that fell off precipitously into a marsh. It was imperative as you were driving to memorize every turnout, every clearing or driveway you passed, anyplace you might back up and pull into if you came upon a vehicle traveling toward you. Local custom provided that the car nearest a turnout would yield; but you could never know if the oncoming driver knew the custom or didn't care. It was not uncommon for one driver to feign ignorance while the other backslid off the road entirely or for two cars to face off in a bumper-to-bumper war of wills, each waiting for the other to blink.

Jonny was reclining on a couch in front of a well-lit fireplace when we arrived. He tinkled the ice cubes in a tall glass of bourbon by way of greeting and urged Marge to fix herself a drink. Patting the cushion next to him for her to sit down, he peered at me with a mystified expression. Marge immediately resumed the morning's conversation, having made what inquiries she was able to on a Saturday afternoon. "There's no provision for grandfathering any of these lots," she said. "People who own them stand to lose their investment."

"Peut-être." He raised his glass in a mock toast to fortune. "C'est la tragédie de vie." He launched into a description of a long lunch he'd had with Sophia Loren at the bar of the Crillon Hotel in Paris in the early 1950s. The apparent connection as far as I could figure out was Marge's long dark hair, which he idly touched while discoursing on the high life he was able to live in France after the Second World War and the authors he'd hung out with. Allen Ginsberg. Gregory Corso. William Burroughs. I was especially taken with his description of the buffet menu at the hotel bar and very aware that I smelled nothing even remotely like dinner cooking.

If Marge was flattered by Jonny's attention, she didn't show it, and remained focused on the problem at hand. "I think we can fight this," she said. "We can organize."

Jonny chuckled at the idea and tossed it off. "Man the barricades. Take it to the selectmen."

But again, Marge was on point. "Not the planning board?"

"Well, then the planning board," he said with little interest, and toddled to the bar to fix himself another drink. Marge had suffered a lot of drunks in her time. She respected Jonny and was enjoying his stories. "Perhaps it's time we ate," she said in a hopeful attempt to salvage the evening.

But Jonny preempted any notion of food with a nostalgic recollection of his favorite Parisian neighborhood, Pigalle, which even I knew was an infamous red light district, and a woman he used to know. "Marie-Lourdes. *Ma fille délicieuse.*" Jonny relished each syllable of her name, his eyelids fluttering, his tongue, like an adder's, flicking the air, all the while inching closer to Marge until his head was lolling on her shoulder, his palm on her knee.

"Look," she said firmly. "I don't really think this is a good idea."

Jonny purred, "Why ever not?"

"Well, for one thing," she lifted his hand from her knee. "My husband is right here."

Jonny sat upright, as if shaken from a dream. Yes, damn it all. There I was indeed. "You're married to her?"

"Bingo." I waved from the corner.

He peered at Marge with a wicked smile. "Perhaps he'd like to join us?"

"Only for dinner," she said.

Jonny sighed, as if this was nothing new to him, and was apparently just getting down to work. "You find me hideous, don't you?"

"Of course not," she said.

"Ah, but you do." His voice was the sympathetic vibration of a well-tuned violin. "You find me detestable, a gruesome deformed freak."

"Not at all," Marge protested, edging off the couch and dropping to a knee. I thought I remembered the same dialog from Jean Cocteau's *Beauty and the Beast*.

"But you do or you would stay." He played it for all he was worth, his voice cracking, his head rolling from side to side in an anguish only deepened by Marge's denials. I realized I was in the presence of a pro. My wife grew up on the streets of inner city Detroit and had lived in Paris, Manhattan, and San Francisco. She had turned away pimps, gropers, jocks, professors, stalkers, flashers, pompous editors, beat poets and particle physicists. But here was the king, the pasha, the irrefutable czar of sex for guilt.

"It's just not going to happen," she said tenderly.

"Because I repulse you." He had managed to expel one enormous teardrop, the size of a soft gel capsule of vitamin e, which twinkled gold in the firelight then disappeared into his beard. "I'm an abomination."

"No, no at all!"

"A feeble cripple with disgusting twisted legs."

"But. . . ," Marge stroked his cheek and uttered a

line I will remember until the day I die, "such a beautiful head."

Jonny lowered his eyelids. He basked in the warmth of the compliment, then thrust his face forward, tongue first, holding her chin in place as he probed her throat with a long wet kiss.

I pulled Marge out the door, down the driveway, back to the car, and reversed full throttle into a mud puddle two feet deep. We took a wrong turn at the pond, came head to head with an oncoming jeep, backed over a log and lost the muffler. The exhaust roared like a chainsaw as we searched the highway for a late-night place to eat. We'd been duped, trapped, and humiliated and silently faced each other across a picnic table, eating greasy hamburgers and swatting mosquitoes with the understanding that this miserable evening was only the prelude to the next. The Selectmen met on Monday. night.

Selectmen are members of a town council. The term originates in eighteenth-century New England, the ascetic home of Puritan repression, Cotton Mather, and the public torture of sexually active women accused of being witches. But within minutes of shyly edging my way into the back of the Board of Selectmen's meeting, I was hooked. It had little to do with the zoning issue; that was quickly referred to the planning board (and eventually Marge did lose much of the worth of those lots). No, it was all about the stories.

I wrote fiction all day every day, creating characters and narrative that couldn't compare to the conflicts that raged before the Board. The most miserable misanthropic hermit in town demands a guarantee that if she collapses in her kitchen only those members of the rescue squad whose names she had scotch taped to her screen door would be granted permission to resuscitate her. There was the man indignant about his arrest for shooting his friend in the foot when the friend insisted he didn't mind being shot and the father who ran naked from the shower to chase the neighbor's pit bull away from his daughter. You could not make this stuff up. The restaurateur arguing that the Senior Center was stealing his business because it served coffee; the mother who refused to come down from a tree on the town green because her children were told by the police not to climb it. I became a regular.

My presence did not go unnoticed. I was considered a fresh young face. The fact that I washed and shaved it regularly was a plus, as was the fact that nobody could actually place it. An election was approaching and in due course I was summoned to a meeting of the town's power brokers, a dozen retired businessmen in their eighties whose politics were so wildly dissimilar that they would never have remained in the same room if they weren't too deaf to hear what the others were saying. I wore my tweed sports coat and a bold rep tie and they eyed me like a suspiciously low-priced used car.

"Gentlemen," I began. "I'm flattered. But I have

to admit that I have no opinions on town matters, no knowledge of town history, and no name recognition."

A long weighty silence ensued during which they came to a consensus. No problem! Everyone else they asked had refused to run.

I was one of five candidates in a race for two open seats. The serious competition consisted of a religious school teacher named Eulalia Hammer and a native born oysterman from one of the oldest families in town. My sole advantage was the fact that the town's demographics were changing and we had one of the largest per capita populations of retirees in the country. The bulk of my supporters were new people in town, former suburbanites retired to live year round in their vacation houses and to them I represented a heartwarming reminder of home, the frizzy-haired Jewish kid who smoked pot with their daughters in the basement.

As to the issues, I was advised to avoid them and concentrate on the one strength that differentiated me from the other candidates, an unctuous desperation to be liked. It turned out that no one actually cared about my political positions, only that I listened to theirs, a strategy antithetical to Mrs. Hammer's, who viewed every question as a rare opportunity to converse with someone more than 10 years old and whose every answer sounded like a warning that Jesus was watching to see if you washed your hands after using the potty. The oysterman was armed with statistics about the environmental damage caused by the building of houses by all the new people in town but this only pissed off all the new people in town, while the natives' attitude was summed up by one old man who said, "All that may be, but your great uncle knocked up my grandpa's sister afore he ran off to World War One, so you can go to hell."

And so I was elected with a large plurality, followed by Mrs. Hammer, and we joined a Board that dedicated itself to reforming town government by humiliating and, when possible, firing everyone who worked for it.

The Board was chaired by an erudite woman with soldierly bearing, Mrs. Flay, the daughter of a Canadian Air Force Major General who dressed herself in a uniform fashioned from an Orvis catalog: red wool blazer, twill slacks and riding boots. At first she seemed to me detached and coolly dispassionate, as on the night she sat at rigid attention in the presence of the totally soused owner of the pit bull. "You're Nazis, all of you!" he railed at the Board. "Can anyone prove those bite marks are from *my* dog's teeth? As soon as that little hypochondriac gets out of intensive care I demand DNA tests, do you hear me?" It had never occurred to me that Mrs. Flay might be as shit-faced as the petitioners themselves until she began to telephone me every evening at happy hour. "Oh, Ira, I do hope you have a moment." Her overture was a breathy supplication, a hostess in a velvet caftan crossing the carpet with a tray of cocktails. Loaded myself by 5:30 in the afternoon, I welcomed these disembodied flirtations, tentative but alive with suggestion, like the accidental brush of a hand on your bottom, as we proceeded to shop the latest town gossip.

In my own work at this time I was fielding a string of rejections for a novel I had begun with the wildest, most entertaining twenty-five pages I had ever written but that, like a fart, began with a bang and progressively diminished in intensity until it left the reader with the faint redolence of cheese. But who needed fiction? I was in the thick of real life drama. If gossipy telephone trysts gave me the opportunity to harmlessly roast people in private, selectmen's meetings were an opportunity to do serious damage. Town employees were routinely reduced to sputtering rages and occasionally tears as Mrs. Hammer used a sublimely sadistic method of attack she had perfected during her years as a religious educator. At one meeting she blandly began questioning Doug Toomy, an ex-heavyweight college wrestler now on the rescue squad. "You were driving down Route Six last night in a town-owned vehicle, weren't you, Doug?"

"I suppose I was, Missus."

"Well, I saw you, Douglas, so there is no need to suppose is there?" Then, with the bashful falsetto of a child hiding behind a curtain, "Why were you breaking the law?"

He slid to the edge of his chair. "I wasn't breaking any law."

"Do we want to tell a lie, Douglas?" She glanced briefly at the ceiling as if to remind him he was standing before an authority even more important than the

Board of Selectmen. "I know you were breaking the law because you passed me while I was driving at the posted speed limit." But she was hardly finished. "What if there had been a child in the road, Douglas?"

Speechless, the large man dropped his eyes to his size thirteen boots.

After Columbus Day the restaurants closed and the boats were pulled from the water. People boarded up their summer businesses and began reading the local newspapers again, delighted with weekly reports of a juicy auto-da-fé. My phone rang constantly with calls from people anxious to tell me stories of municipal waste and gross misconduct. At happy hour I could count on Mrs. Flay's latest cocktail gossip.

To put this in perspective, my most popular novel, *The Kitchen Man*, came out to rave reviews, sold mass market and foreign rights, and was optioned to Universal Pictures. Of the number of people I interacted with on a daily basis, only a handful knew I had even written a book and the rest viewed it as less interesting than an angry letter to the editor. As a selectman I was in the news every week. Decisions I made were immediately enacted by staff as opposed to novels that took years to write before moving glacially through one editorial committee after another. I was the boss, not a petitioner at the mercy of an agent or editor. I got paid regularly; a pittance, but no publisher ever kept up my health insurance. The truth was that I was happier as a small town politician than I had ever been as a writer. Before long I had the friendships that had eluded me when I first moved to town, almost all of them made through town government.

Porter Dudley, the new Town Administrator, hired in my third year of office, was the closest. After we reduced his predecessor to a quaking mass of facial tics, we earned a reputation as a town without pity, the kind of quaint New England village described in stories like "The Lottery." Although our advertisement offered a competitive salary, few applicants wanted a job that would end in a Moscow show trial. Dudley was the best of the crop. He was not experienced but worked the job night and day to get up to speed, offering a sympathetic ear to people who felt they'd never had a voice.

He spoke incessantly about his kids and his wife— to whom he wrote rhymed verse, which he insisted on showing me when he discovered my wife was a poet. His family still lived in Ohio until he could afford to bring them east. Therefore most evenings found him at the local pub where he was nicknamed Old Port and played darts with the fishermen, many of whom I had barely known until Dudley introduced us.

A short rubber-faced man with loose jowls and a flat, misshapen nose, Dudley was a great storyteller, a compassionate listener, and a mimic who did impressions. He did a police sergeant pulling up his pants as he chased after a skate boarder. He did the recreation director, pumping his fist after beating a 9-year-old in tennis. He did me, the way I got bored and sleepy at meetings and slouched, my legs splayed, my butt slipping so far down the chair that I might have been doing the limbo. He did Mrs. Flay and her breathy, patronizing voice: his fatal mistake and one that reached her with viral speed.

The Chairwoman had never liked Porter Dudley. He was a begrudging choice from a poor pool of applicants and from the beginning she had dubbed him "Any Port in a Storm." She preferred professionals with impressive degrees and crisp wool suits. Dudley was just too common a man for her to respect but more to the point, too well liked. He replaced her in the eyes of the people as the most important person in town. Even when a letter appeared in the newspaper praising him, she called him Dudley Do-right. In time she began to repeat rumors in our nightly cocktail conversations. "Oh, Ira, I hear that he returns from lunch at the pub quite tipsy every day."

The Board of Selectman's meetings became a star chamber in which his petty oversights were exaggerated to enormous proportion. One night Eulalia Hammer cross-examined him about a light bulb. "Mr. Dudley, I happened to drive down to the harbor the other night and I was shocked to find it dark in front of the harbormaster's building."

"Probably a bulb needs changing. I'll see to it."

In her most angelic voice: "What if a child had been down there?"

"That was how late, Ma'am? In the off-season? What would a child be doing down at the harbor?"

"Well, what if a little boy was in the car with his

grandfather? And what if his grandfather had a heart attack? And what if a violent pedophile had escaped from the state prison for the criminally insane that day?"

Dudley began to sweat. "Is this a likely scenario, Madame Chair?" But Mrs. Flay sat at military attention, her shoulders as square as the uprights of a guillotine, her gaze looming over him like a blade.

It is a cold and soggy night in early December and except for the spinning tires of an occasional pickup, the distant yelps of a coyote pack in the marsh, there isn't a hint of life on Main Street. Even the teenagers have abandoned the bench in front of Town Hall. Through the tall windows in the conference room a fluorescent lamp casts its wan blue light over five tired people sitting at an old oak table, four of them determined to end a man's career, me opposed. There is no audience tonight. There are no reporters. An executive session has been called, closed to the public, for the alleged purpose of discussing contract negotiations, but there is very little discussion and no negotiating, only accusations of Dudley's ineptitude without Dudley present to defend himself—in my eyes a violation of the Open Meeting Law. Although Hammer and Flay and the other two Selectmen have the votes they need to refuse to extend Dudley's contract, they know he is popular and they crave a unanimous decision. My negative vote is the one pitiful claim to power I have left. It is fifteen minutes to midnight and we have been inhaling each other's rancid breath since six. Mrs.

Flay makes a last tired plea, "Oh, Ira, admit it, he's a loser." Once again she reads off the litany of his offenses. "You have to admit he's incompetent."

I didn't think he was anything of the kind. The snow got plowed. The garbage got collected. The rescue squad got people to the hospital. Were we selling off mineral rights? Bombing innocent civilians? Sending indigent teenage soldiers off to fight and die? In comparison to the federal government this little town was the kingdom of heaven.

The vote was taken at five minutes past midnight. It was decided that Dudley's contract would not be renewed and that no announcement need be given the press. Once advised that he was about to be canned, Dudley would have no option that would save his reputation but to quietly resign.

Mrs. Flay waved a friendly good-bye as we hustled to our cars, the moist air cooling to hoar frost, the parking lot slippery with black ice, and I was confronted with one of those movie moments, when the sound track gives way to the slow beating of the heart and there is an important decision to be made, usually in tight close-up, a choice in which true character is tested. For instance, I could admit my loss, make peace with the others on the board, or back over her with my truck. An easy decision. I returned her wave. But the choices kept presenting themselves.

I could either discuss the situation with my wife when I returned home, take the opportunity to calmly face the fact that I was powerless to save my friend's job—or close myself off with the TV on and a bottle of scotch. I filled a glass with ice.

I could come up with a strategy that would work for the benefit of the town, leverage my role as the Board's conscience to negotiate a good settlement package for Dudley. Or, I could call the reporters and blow the whistle, expose their covert little cabal to the light of day.

This was the most difficult decision to make and one that, in my addled state of mind at least, was strangely paralleled by a bizarre story unfolding on CNN Newsroom. A Midwestern teenager, an honor student, had been caught cheating for his final exams. As punishment, his father, a minister, decreed that he was barred from attending the senior prom. Unaccountably identifying with the kid, I imagined the choices running through his mind. He could try to talk with his father and work out an alternate punishment. He could beg for mercy. He could run away from home. Instead, according to Wolf Blitzer, he calmly broke into the living room gun cabinet, loaded a pump action shot gun, and blew the old man's face off at close range.

Why this story resonated was a mystery to me. Only a psychopath would be driven to murder because he was docked from the prom, only an unstable, catastrophic mind unable to accept a decision he could not control. Certainly no normal person could be driven to this extreme. Unless you found yourself in a situation in which you were thoroughly convinced there is no alternative;

that a malicious injury has taken place; that if the people responsible are not stopped they will simply do it again, to you and to others, forever more, with impunity. Once you begin to think this way you may very well be prone to making a decision you will regret.

I called the reporters.

Two hundred people crammed into a meeting room built for half that number. Those who couldn't find chairs crowded the aisles. An angry mob gathered in back. Many more stamped their feet in the cold, watching through the windows thrown open in spite of the Chairwoman's order to close them. The town was at war. Dudley's supporters, some of whom had never been to a meeting before, and others who knew him as a fine dart player but were surprised to discover he was the Town Administrator, pumped their fists and demanded answers.

The Chairwoman shuffled her papers, afraid to face the crowd. "We request that due to the impossibility of addressing everyone's concerns here tonight people will please frame their questions in the form of a letter."

"Yeah, and you'll find it through your window tomorrow morning wrapped around a rock!" The outburst was affirmed by a loud series of rhythmic hoots. The old wooden floor shook. Meetings, the newcomers in the audience discovered, could be fun.

Now frightened for her safety, Mrs. Flay requested a side meeting with the police chief who duly radioed for backup. My decision to alert the press had fomented the show of support for Dudley and frankly it was difficult not to gloat. But I had decided to exercise magnanimity. I raised my hand to read aloud a call for healing. The Chairwoman looked straight through me and duly recognized a friend of hers from the audience, who stood up to read a letter she had posted to the district attorney.

"Madame Chair, we believe that Massachusetts General Law has been breached, and we cite Penalties for Violation of Confidentiality. May I go on?"

The color returned to Mrs. Flay's cheeks. She suddenly looked hopeful. "Oh, yes, do go on."

The letter reader detailed a significant penalty. "A fine of up to $100,000. . . ."

Did I hear one hundred *thousand* dollars? For violation of *what*?

". . . and imprisonment of up to two years. . . ."

Imprisonment? For calling a couple of reporters?

"Madame Chair, we intend to take this to the highest levels."

"Well, I would hope you would." Mrs. Flay nodded sincere agreement. "A breach of the sanctity of the executive session is a serious offense, not to mention the privacy of Mr. Dudley who must certainly be considering a civil suit against whoever leaked the information."

Dudley file a lawsuit? Suddenly *he* looked hopeful. But I had tried to help him.

"We will not rest until the mole is exposed and punished." The letter reader looked directly at me. "One of you has disgraced this town in the eyes of the public and ruined the reputation of an innocent man."

"Ira?" The voice was Mrs. Flay's. "Ira?" Sweat was seeping from my hairline and collecting in my ears. "Ira?" she repeated sweetly. "Did you have something you wanted to read?"

I managed to shake my head in the negative and pocket my carefully crafted speech. My face was hot with fever. My arms and legs were numb. I had no idea if what I had done had any legal implications but my imagination played host to a catastrophic array of police interviews, cross examination, and criminal litigation. In a pique of rage I had compromised a legally consti- tuted executive session. In the eyes of the dart players I might be a hero, a whistle-blower; but in the confident smiles of Hammer and Flay, I was the new target and my action the perfect decoy for theirs.

Newspaper reporters whom I had not called, angry at having been scooped by the ones I had, now worked to expose the rat. Dudley, having no idea where the leak had come from, hired counsel to pursue a civil action for disclosure of information relating to his employ- ment. Passions were divided between Dudley loyalists and those who sought vindication for Hammer and Flay. Arguments broke out at the post office, businesses were boycotted subject to their owners' opinions; some- one claimed his tires were slashed. It was not uncom- mon for people who had known each other for years to push their supermarket carts straight past each other without a word. Mrs. Flay demanded police protection. Everyone, however, wanted to discover the identity of the snitch.

It is hard to disappear in a village but I tried. I shopped out of town. I went for my mail at five minutes before closing. I called in sick to meetings. I had dreams of my home being raided at 4 A.M. by surly federal agents in blue wind breakers, of shuffling to court in shackles and running a gauntlet of reporters and protestors who prodded me with signs and chanted slogans about the sanctity of executive session minutes.

Although it was months before I stopped jumping at the sound of the ringing telephone, no action was ever taken. Nonetheless, I had lost the stomach for politics and public life, even reading the local papers. On those rare nights when I could relax enough to sleep, it was only by visualizing the stagnant silence of a paper-strewn office, the innumerable trips to the bathroom, the futile search through the refrigerator for lunch, the mailbox full of rejections, the telephone that never rang, the dusty pile of old *New Yorker* magazines that beckoned from the rack beside the toilet; in effect, the tedious life of the mid-list writer and the sublime futility of knowing that as a novelist at the beginning of the twentieth-first century I was blissfully invisible and all but irrelevant to the world.

HEARTSONG OF THE WARRIOR, INC.

We were ordered to report on a Saturday morning at 8 A.M. By eight-thirty over a hundred men were stomping their feet in the mid-December cold, pounding on the gray metal doors and shouting curses at the red brick facade of the old school building. An argument over a parking space had already turned into a shoving match, a couple of guys were playing keep away with a shorter guy's hat and I started to think that if they kept us out here much longer this was going to turn into something out of *Lord of the Flies*.

As the bitter wind gathered force over the playing fields, I pulled my watch cap low over my ears and turned my expression to stone, determined to appear tough and inscrutable.

Two faces peered at us through the wire mesh windows of the auditorium. Sporadic outbursts of grumbling grew into waves of rage and at 8:45 a rebellious spin-off group began kicking the doors. "Open up, you bastards."

"It's freezing out here! Let us in."

"Let us in! Let us in!" A small crowd picked up the chant.

One guy took a running start with a trashcan and used it as a battering ram. A flurry of ice balls pelted the windows. A man in a leather jacket climbed on a concrete balustrade to address the crowd. "Is this what we're paying for? To be treated like animals?" He threw his cigarette to the ground and stormed back to the parking lot, loudly announcing, "I am the fuck out of here!"

"Very smart," said a man behind me. He was no more than five-foot-three and wore a Sherpa cap from Nepal with earflaps and a long red tassel.

"Not so smart," I said. "The deposit's not refundable."

"Oh, he'll just sit in his car with the heater on until they open the doors. I'm talking about Golden, the organizer. He's brilliant. He trained with Werner. He's already weeding out the leaders from the followers. In most workshops it takes hours." Arms folded across his thick Guatemalan sweater, he did a little jig every few minutes to stay warm. "I think you're going to get what you paid for."

"Pneumonia?"

His half smile was an expression of patience. "In *Finding the Shaman Within* they herded us into a freezing lake."

"Somebody could have had a heart attack."

He nodded as if remembering it fondly.

If I hadn't sunk $500 into "the training" I would have headed back to my own car and home. Had I actually believed I'd learn to "connect with the lost masculine power within?" I knew it was all a crock back at the free introductory evening (cost to be applied to tuition) when we were lectured by a hirsute jock spouting dialog straight out of *Dances with Wolves*. Est, primal therapy, Transcendental Meditation, The Forum: just like this one, scams every one, I knew it, cults, quick-fix fads. But I simply didn't know where else to turn. I hadn't been in a fight since the lunch line in junior high when some nitwit stuck me in the butt with the needle of a drawing compass and I kicked him in the kneecap and ran. Now I was forty years older, my lip split, my face bludgeoned, two stitches in my eyebrow, and I mailed off a check in the hope of learning "to become the man I always wanted to be."

When the doors finally opened we poured into an overheated hallway smelling of floor polish and chalk. Men in white shirts and pants and identical brown vests herded us into a single line, shouted instructions, and ordered us not to speak. My little friend did not rush into the building with the others but lingered at my side. "At least we're out of the wind," I said, when a thick palm dropped on my shoulder. "Are you deaf? Zip it up. No talking."

Waiting until he passed, I whispered. "What kind of bull shit is this?"

"It's a little like *The Inner Path of the Wayfinder*." My

friend sounded impressed. "They physically restrained people in that one. Tied them up in the dark for a few hours until they cried for help. The key is to locate your personal level of fear. Where does your ego stop and the true courage within you begin?"

"Tied them up in the dark?"

An enormous block of a man strode straight for us. He had a wide protruding forehead that cast his eyes in shadow and wore a cheap toupee with sideburns, like a helmet made of stiff brown hair. "Knit your lips, Asshole."

"Talking to me?" I asked.

"Who else?"

The entire line of men awaited my response. Would I stand firm? Shout back? Run? My little mentor lowered his eyes and placed his palms together, willing me to hold my tongue. What the fuck was I doing here?

I'd had the fight over a month and a half ago. My wife and I were in the car, returning from the annual Oyster Festival. Town was full of partying tourists but the only thing on my mind was the screenplay I'd recently submitted, the final draft, on schedule to the day, and that I hadn't heard a word from the producer. It had been over three weeks and I had to assume she hated it, that the script upon which I had based my hopes of a screenwriting career was not only bad but beneath comment. My entire weekend was tension amped to near hysteria. I had no appetite. I couldn't concentrate. Driving the country road back from town I noticed a car following too close. He flashed his hi-beams. I tapped my brakes. He blasted his horn. I dropped my speed. He screamed out the window. When I flipped him the bird he tapped my bumper. When I pulled off the road, he drew up behind me. "Where are you going?" Marge grabbed my sleeve as the doors of the car behind us flew open. "Get back in the car!" she screamed.

We were marched into a classroom with eight long tables. Helmet hair handed each of us a release form. I AGREE THAT UNDER NO CIRCUMSTANCES WILL I HOLD THE INSTITUTE LIABLE FOR PHYSICAL OR PSYCHOLOGICAL DAMAGE. We were further prohibited from publically divulging any aspect of the training and requested to list the names of our physician, closest living relative, health care proxy, incidence of heart failure, and blood type (if known).

I glanced apprehensively to my side.

"In *Empowering the Inner Shape-shifter*," my friend whispered, "masked men held us at gunpoint."

Long green shades were drawn across the gymnasium skylights to block out the mid-morning sun and we were ordered to stand at military attention as the thugs in brown vests strode between our ranks and pushed us into uniform rows. Anyone who spoke was dragged out of line. One guy insisted on using the bathroom and was not allowed back in. It was standard large group awareness training, of course. Harass people, break them down, make them feel helpless, and then reverse the process. In fact, it was textbook, the same bogus technique they used in revival meetings. Once the entire group was in despair the leader gave them hope. Everyone experienced a collective endorphin high and was softened up to receive "the message," whatever crap they were serving. After standing in line for over an hour, I felt a kind of kinship with the guys around me, as if we were all inmates in the prison yard. We whispered jokes about the "guards" sotto voce and passed around a contraband package of gum. After another hour of shouting orders, Helmet hair barked, "At ease," and everyone started talking at once.

"What's your name?" I asked my friend.

He gave a short disdainful laugh. "It's not the name we're given but the deeper meaning we reveal about ourselves." He stared at my forehead, at the stitch marks that cut a deep jagged gorge through my eyebrow, already forming a permanent scar, then shrugged, as if to say forget it, you're learning. "I'm Green-Forest," he said.

"Glad to meet you, Green."

"Green-Forest," he corrected me. "My last name is Everyhuman."

A long limbed and willowy man wearing harem pants whipped around. "You're Green-Forest Everyhuman?"

Green-Forest brought his palms together and lowered his chin to his fingertips.

"I met you in *Dance of the Spirit Walker*."

"And you call yourself. . . . "

"River Freebody."

They threw their arms above their heads, made an

arch with the flats of their hands, swirled around beneath it, took a step backward and bowed. River Freebody gave me a hard look. "Did we meet at Omega? Circumcision?"

Could he tell? Did it matter?

"He means the workshop," Green-Forest explained. "*Circumcision Healing: Reconnecting With Our Loss.*"

A drumbeat, a far-off pounding at first like the throbbing of a wild beast's heart, came close, closer still. Bop-BOM. Bop-BOM. Soon another drum joined in. Bop-bop-BOM-bop. Bop-bop-BOM-bop. Then another drum and another until the entire room seemed to vibrate and then above it all came the shrill cry of a man in pain.

"Brothers! Warriors, help me!" the voice beseeched us. "I am dying!" followed by a cry of agony more wrenching than the first. "In the midst of battle I die alone. Blinded by my enemies, I wander the earth alone." His cry was piercing. I was not the only one who felt it. The entire group was searching for the wounded man in pain.

Blue spotlights came up on a dark stage. A smoke machine cranked out an eerie mist. Long fat sticks of incense glowed like torches. A stout naked man stepped into the circle of light.

Green-Forest leapt up, ecstatic. "It's Golden!"

"Golden . . . what?"

"Harvey Morris Golden. The workshop leader. Shh-hh. . . ."

He was a round boulder of a man wearing a loincloth made of fur. I thought of a sumo wrestler as he lifted his heavy thighs. His pectorals, once muscle, rested flat on his belly like an old woman's breasts. But sumo wrestlers shaved their skin while Golden's was a thick mat of curly black hair. "Where is my tribe?" His voice was an impassioned incantation that cracked for effect like a cantor singing *Kol Nidre*. "For decades I have searched. Once we were intrepid hunters! Once we walked the earth together in strength! Once we left the women to their planting and gathering and trekked the earth with our elders for game. Now we turn our backs on our brothers. And we die alone."

"You're not alone!" Green-Forest shouted.

"Once we spoke in council. Once we fought our enemies back to back. But now we are weak." For over an hour he lambasted us with our failures. We failed to raise our young. We failed to take responsibility. We gave our lives to our work, to girlfriends, to the internet, to the media, to every meaningless pursuit modern culture had to offer and ignored each other. Each of us was alone. Each of us was in pain. I was dizzy from standing so long, from breathing incense. My eyes were stinging from smoke. Golden talked for another hour and what seemed another, haranguing us with shame until he fell silent, hung his head and raised his arms to the sky. "Where are my brothers?" he moaned. "Will you let me die alone?"

"No!" Green-Forest rushed the stage. River Freebody

163

sprinted up the aisle "No! No!" A mass of men followed until Golden was surrounded, a large animal swarmed by its wriggling young. "Feel our strength!" Golden's voice rose above the basketball hoops and echoed among the banners that read Division One Champions. "Feel our strength!"

Bop-BOM-bom-bom. Bop-BOM-bom-bom. The drumbeat resumed. Green-Forest tore off his sweater and waved it above his head. He kicked off his Ugg boots and wriggled from his pants. What the fuck was going on here? Soon every guy in the room was scrambling out of his clothing, tossing it above his head not caring where it landed, or carrying it to the foot of the bleachers and folding it in a neat pile on top of his shoes.

I jumped when River Freebody tugged at my shirt.

"Join us," he said.

"But my keys, my wallet."

"Are you held back by your possessions? Are you defined by your clothing?" He mocked the imprint on my jeans. "Is your name Calvin Klein? Did your forefathers not stalk the wild prey while wearing the skins of animals?"

"I don't know." The shouting. The drums. The fumes of incense were overwhelming. "They were from a *shtetl* near Minsk."

"If you fear weakness, we'll be your strength."

Now they were spinning in circles, now they were dancing. Naked men dancing, how pitiful was this? Flabby men, frail men; men of all ages. One with shriveled legs bobbed in sync to the drumbeat while sitting in his wheel chair; another, who looked to be 90 years old, wore only a stained undershirt, his long scrotum swaying like a water balloon. As the gym swelled with body heat and the odor of sweat, I only knew that I didn't fall for this kind of theater. I wanted out. It was all a humiliating charade. I cursed myself again for having been taken in. Maybe it was modesty, or pride, or fear. Maybe it was just as Golden said, I was doomed to wander alone in the desert. Whatever, I didn't want any part of it.

When their games began, I took off my shoes, my socks, my shirt, but no matter how loud I cheered or how fast I ran, kicking the plastic buffalo skull across the gym floor, I knew I was faking it. I could never be one of them.

Green-Forest appeared through a cloud of smoke. "Trust your body, Man of Deep Scars. The mind deceives."

"Man of Deep Scars?"

"That's who you are, isn't it?" He lightly touched the bruise on my forehead and waited as I fingered the buckle of my belt. I dropped my pants, my underwear. If I looked no more asinine than any other fool it was small consolation.

The games continued until the sun went down and the gym was a mass of shadow. The evening feast was served around a ritual fire. In another age men shared the carcasses of the hunt but the majority of the men here, we were informed, had checked off a preference for vegetarian on the application form and now we sat around the glowing embers of a lava coal gas grill from Sears, passing heads of cabbage which each brave warrior dipped in a communal vat of Russian dressing, chewed with grunts of satisfaction, and washed down with diet cola served in souvenir plastic mugs imprinted with the name of Golden's institute, *Heartsong of the Warrior, Inc.*

After the meal, Golden stood in the middle of our circle waving a long crooked stick laced with rawhide and feathers. "We have kept our pain from one another for too long," he said. "It is time to unlock the secrets. It is time to heal our wounds instead of hiding them. Who has courage among you, Warriors? Who has the courage to bare your wounds?"

The naked tribe settled around him, sitting cross-legged or squatting on their haunches in silent anticipation. The big chief was calling for his braves to pierce their skin and release the spirit, to puncture their defenses, he said, like shards of bone through the flesh. "*Wakan tanan kici un*!" he cried.

"*Wakan tanan kici un*!" they responded.

"The wounds of the battlefield, Warriors! Battles with wives, with mothers, with lovers! Battles in business! Family battles! Money battles! Sexual battles! *Wakan tanan kici un*! May the Great Spirit bless you! Share and heal." He threw down the stick. "Share and heal."

A soft murmur began. "Share and heal. Share and heal," until the words were no longer English but some transcendental ritual chant. I was searching instinctively for the exits when River Freebody broke to the center of the circle in tears.

"I was married to a woman for fourteen years," he began. "I worked my way from associate to junior partner. To make money for her! She said we weren't spending enough time together, so I bought a home theater package. For her! She said I didn't know my kids, so I built a pool in the backyard. I spared nothing to make her happy. Nothing! She said I didn't excite her in bed so I had a hair transplant. And out of nowhere, after fourteen years, with no warning. . . . " His voice cracked. The veins in his neck constricted, tight as the roots of a tree. He started to shake. Three men rushed to hold him up. "She walked out on me. She said it was over. Over!" he wailed, and sank to his knees.

"It's from soap operas!" one guy cried out. "They get it from watching soaps all day."

"It's the feminists," came another voice.

Share and heal! Share and heal! The drumbeat resumed.

"I. . . ." A man stood up, voice quavering. "I. . . ."

Share and heal! Share and heal!

"I can't get it up with my wife anymore!"

"Who can?" came the response from the dark.

"That doesn't mean I'm less of a man!"

"No! No!" came the response. "We love you, Brother!"

If I was supposed to identify with this binge of self-pity it wasn't working. I felt trapped in the middle of a testosterone-soaked encounter group, except that I couldn't deny their nerve, their audacious willingness to share the most embarrassing secrets of their lives. Clearly the price of entrance to the tribe, however bogus the notion, was the courage to speak the unspoken and one guy after another strode to the center of the circle, astonishing me with his ability to do just that. What they got out of it I couldn't say but even as I inched to the edges of the crowd, I remained transfixed by the spectacle.

I could never risk the ridicule, and even if I tried, what did I have to offer? What were my petty troubles compared to a son's guilt for refusing to visit his mother with Alzheimer's? Compared to the anguish of a man who had been abused by his grandfather for years? Another who had fathered his own brother's child?

"Man of Deep Scars!" It was Green-Forest, calling me that idiotic name. "Man of Deep Scars! What are you hiding?"

Share and heal! Share and heal! It was me they were looking at, calling me out.

River Freebody took my right arm and Green-Forest my left, leading me to the center of the circle. Even if I wanted to speak, I couldn't. Spill my guts to a gym full of naked strangers? Ridiculous. But they were watching me, waiting. It was a setup, plain as day. It was a cowardly act *not* to speak. I had to give them something, anything. "I was addicted to coke!" I yammered. "I spent thousands of dollars of our savings on coke." But they scoffed at that. It meant nothing to them.

"Hope it was good shit!"

"Got a toot for a Bro?"

I didn't know what they wanted. I hadn't fucked up in some major, dramatic way that deserved sympathy. My problems were the plaints of a middle class neurotic. I hadn't published a book in years, big deal. I was a small town political hack, a compulsive backyard gardener preoccupied with sex. Everything about me was medio-cre, including my failures. Sweat collected in the corners of my eyes. My forehead felt about to explode.

I had to get out of this. Who cared what these losers thought? "I don't make shit for money, okay! I live off my wife! She supports us, all right! My wife supports us!" It was out. I had said it.

"That's all you got, Scarface?"

"What's her number, man?"

"Whose wife don't work? Mine has three jobs."

They'd given up on me by now. They were waiting for the next guy to take the stage. I was off the hook. I had passed with a C. I could stroll out of the spotlight un-noticed, dismissed. They actually thought I was afraid of their orgy of self-pity. Frankly I didn't give a fuck what they thought. "I GOT THE SHIT BEAT OUT ME IN A FIGHT, OKAY?" That got their attention.

"We could see that all right!" came a voice from the dark.

But they didn't see it and they didn't feel the fist hit my face or the echo in my head like a metal cage clanging. They didn't see the bigger man's proud little dance step as I staggered backward, tasting blood as I bit through my tongue, or my wife running from the car, flailing her arms with a high-pitched scream. They didn't feel my shame as I tripped and fell and tried to get to my feet as another man, the guy's son, ran at me from my blind side and kicked me in the head. "BUT THE ONLY REASON I DIDN'T GET HURT WORSE. . . ."

There wasn't a sound in the crowded room now, just their faces on mine, watching me, and the billowing smoke of the incense. I felt weak, hollow except for the shame that seemed to fill me, even my lungs, and I gulped for air as that morning came back to me, the cars slowing on the side of the road, the gawkers gathering to watch two tall men advancing on a much smaller one and a tiny woman forcing her way between. Marge advanced on the father—a mass of sunburned fat and muscle in a tight polo shirt, three times her size—her fists up ready to battle, as he cursed the crazy woman and turned away, called his son off me and back to the car and drove off in an angry cloud of noise and sand. "SHE SAVED ME, ALL RIGHT. I WAS IN A FUCKING FIGHT AND GOT MY ASS KICKED AND THE ONLY REASON I WASN'T HURT WORSE WAS BECAUSE MY WIFE TOOK THE GUY ON! MY WIFE!"

I don't know how I looked to them or sounded and I no longer cared. There were no words left to say. My shoulders were shaking. My throat burned. It was out, I had told it, all of it, and I'd had enough of this degrading spectacle and every fool who took part. I was simply ashamed, of the incident, of having degraded myself by telling it, of being here at all. I wanted out of this circus and I took off for the exit.

But Helmet hair stepped square in front of me and would not let me pass. His head tilted and his hard expression seemed to thaw. "Brother!" He enveloped me in bear hug and within seconds a mass of men was encircling us, climbing our shoulders, jumping up and down. They only backed off to let one through. It was Golden, who drew me into a naked embrace. He smelled like sawdust and beef stew. "I have come to honor your bravery," he said. I was a member of the tribe.

The war dance began or more like it a mosh pit in a *schvitz* bath. *Wakan tanan kici un*! *Wakan tanan kici un*! We careened like bumper cars and threw ourselves into each other's arms until Golden took the stage and silenced us for his final benediction. Flabby arms stretched wide, Moses on Mount Sinai, his voice ricocheted off the cinder block walls of the gym. "Alone we are weak. Alone we are condemned to walk the earth in pain. Together, Warriors, we share strength far beyond our number. We are invincible! We are men of POWER!"

The gym doors burst open. "Power! Power! Power! Power!" we shouted, running naked across the frozen soccer field. It was four o'clock in the morning. The porch lights of the surrounding suburban homes clicked on. Clouds of wood smoke billowed above the goal posts where a smoldering bed of lava stones lay ready for the fire walk. Arms linked, we were numb to fear and welcomed the pain. We had dipped a quill pen in chicken blood and inscribed our e-mail addresses on the sacred mailing list. We had shared our shame. We had committed to meet monthly in small tribal councils for bowling and beer. We were no longer solitary wanderers on the desolate battlefields of the modern world. We were warriors. We were brothers.

Jacked up as I'd been after surviving the barefoot run over coals they told us were 1000 degrees Fahrenheit, the whole thing seemed shameful the next day and left me feeling vaguely queasy, like a hangover after a toga party. A workshop claiming to offer the wisdom of a warrior, or even more embarrassing, believing you've received it, is only an ersatz experience, like claiming a knowledge of French culture after visiting the France Pavilion at Epcot.

But the guys I'd met that weekend and at the regular "powwows" since were real. Teachers. Salesmen. Construction workers. Some who were struggling to find work. A lot of ordinary guys as well as a filmmaker, a physicist, a defense attorney, the winner of a Pulitzer Prize: types I'd always imagined had it made. Most had serious personal problems, trouble with their kids, with sex, with addiction. One guy, an award-winning tri-athlete and former professional bike racer, hid his illiteracy. Others were so hopelessly obvious you wondered how they didn't embarrass themselves: a Boston neurosurgeon who talked obsessively about the lap dancer who really loved him, an heir to a well-known fortune who bemoaned the agony of being born rich. We all had regrets. Every single one of us envied someone else in the group for something he lacked. All of us, to the man, were something shy of what we had imagined ourselves becoming.

But the fact is, I felt perfectly at home. I fit in, just one more sorry-assed loser trying to get by. I wasn't substantially better or worse off than any of the guys I'd met. A surprisingly comforting thought and one that had never occurred to me: failure was normal. How fabulous was that?

The MacArthur Foundation of Vegetables

The producer was visiting my house. My house! No mere story editor two years out of NYU, she was the executive creative assistant vice president of production for a company whose last film had starred Al Pacino. Al Pacino! She had optioned my novel and hired me to write the screenplay. She liked it and after endless drafts and a year of shopping it around she had found a studio that was interested. Since she was visiting family on Cape Cod I suggested we take a meeting at my house.

The movie business was all about relationships, my agent said. Deals are precarious. You had to think long term. I was out of the Hollywood loop, of course, and fashioned myself an image inspired by a Jim Harrison interview: the screenwriter who chooses not to live in LA, the talent indifferent to the game. Part literary outsider, part gentleman farmer. I put it all together: old jeans and boots, oysters with a vintage Chassagne Montrachet for lunch. An old pick-up truck and a big garden. The one thing that worried me, however, the flaw I could not allow my producer to see—My producer!—was weeds. I have a thing about weeds.

She was scheduled to arrive on a Saturday afternoon in June. Before leaving for a month-long research trip to France we had planted our entire garden and returned four days in advance of the her visit to a choking biomass of weeds—stitchwort, dog lichen, toadflax, knotgrass, chickweed, mattress straw, speedwell—overflowing the paths, climbing the fences, suffocating the cucumbers and the peas.

I think of weeds as thugs, the violent underclass of the garden. I think of weeds as gangbangers using their size and numbers to intimidate innocent vegetables. Left to thrive, allowed to spread, to plunder the nutrients of the slow-to-mature tomato, to ravage the fragile hot pepper, the spindly eggplant staggering under its heavy load, these malicious deadbeats leave only destruction and blight in the wake of their hateful creep. Not on my watch!

I began the attack at dawn on the morning after we returned, armed with a stirrup hoe and a hori-hori knife, unearthing pernicious green carpets of chickweed. Midway through the day, however, it began to rain and kept at it for the better part of the week and every square foot I cleared gave birth to more weeds like replacement troops pushing each other to the front, a new one sprouting as soon as I turned my back. After three more days of hacking weeds and hauling them to the dump I broke out the propane-fueled vapor torch and burned my way down every path till dark.

To my mind there is no escaping it. Your garden reveals who you are. If you're a lazy slacker who likes fresh tomatoes but can't even be bothered to mow the lawn, you force a few tomato plants in a pot on your porch. If you're an obsessive compulsive you dig uniform paths between each row, measured to the inch. If you're a geek you lay a grid work of soaker hoses as intricate as a subway map all connected to a digital timer. Likewise people afraid of wildlife protect their garden with a battery of horse rattles, whirligigs, reflector ribbons, tethered beach balls and at least one Styrofoam owl decoy. The worst of the lot are people like me, narcissistic control freaks for whom the garden is an ever-humbling reminder of our inability to impose our will and direction on the world. Yet every St. Patrick's Day, be it above freezing or below, be there sun or rain or a coating of snow which I dutifully shovel off—or ice, which I attack with a pick axe—I plant the peas. Why do I put myself through it?

Because I do my best thinking in the garden.

For years I lived in Cambridge, Massachusetts, a small city home to a large number of famous writers. Nearby there lived a world famous novelist who I would see walking his dog every day. But rather than walking the animal, he seemed to be trailing it aimlessly down to the Charles and up to Harvard Square, his eyes to the ground, barely holding the slack leather leash. The more I encountered him, the more interested I became in his books and over time I read most of them. In the way you do after becoming involved in a writer's work, and therefore in his sensibility if not the facts of his life, you begin to think you know things about him. You know he likes cooking, for instance, because there are recipes in every book. You know that he comes from the working class; and that he sympathizes with feminists. Because many of his sensibilities were my own I was determined to make his acquaintance. I was furthermore not going to approach him like a crass fan, "Hi, I love your work," but as a colleague, and one day I stopped squarely in front of him and said, "Hi, do you mind if I ask you a question?"

"Yes, I actually do," he said, not breaking step. "I'm working."

It took me some time to understand the encounter as a lesson rather than a brush-off. A writer's work entails a great deal of doing nothing at all obvious, or at least nothing to do with making words appear on paper. A writer has to allow the mind itself to wander aimlessly. Some do it tottering behind a dog. Some do it in the bathtub. I learned a long time ago that most of what I forced myself to write was junk and that I needed to stop forcing myself, to allow ideas to arrive or not, like dreams in sleep. For me those ideas come when I'm behind a roto-tiller, or stringing beanpoles, or moving clumps of day lilies. When the ideas don't come, which is most of the time, fuck it all, at least the day lilies get moved.

Because it's better than a rowing machine.

I think I'm overweight (and you probably think you are, too). Therefore seven months out of the year I torment myself for about an hour every day on exercise machines. Over the years I have tried treadmills, stair masters, bicycles, ellipticals, universal gyms, free weights, stability balls, resistance tubing, and have settled on the Nordic-Trak cross-county ski machine because it is the most painful. I also own a state-of-the-art Concept2 rowing machine but I don't use it as a rule because I enjoy it and therefore don't believe it could possibly be doing me as much good. Working out on these machines bothers me, however, because it seems a total waste of energy, like a furnace pumping hot air through a vacant house.

I once had a high school science teacher who made his children power their television set with a stationary bicycle attached to a generator. However parsimonious this seemed at the time, it does strike me as a reasonable way to make use of a worthless expenditure of foot-pounds. I might have shopped for such a generator except that there's too much equipment in my bedroom already. Half the time just making her way to the bed for sex my wife bashes her shins on the rowing machine (it is nine feet long) and we've found it is not erotic to wait for swelling to go down. Nor do I like what working out does to my mind. Because it is boring to exercise in my bedroom, I have devised any number of ways to enliven the experience. MP3s on my Droid phone work well. NFL football games are very good. Until it was cancelled the all-time best was the Fox series *24*, which made my heart race and my blood bubble but messed with my politics and turned me into a sweat-soaked overweight vigilante in spandex shorts chasing terrorists on a stationary ski machine while shouting, "Down that alley, Jack! Get him! GET HIM!"

In the spring of every year, however, we use the machines to hang our clothes on and get our exercise in the garden where the term "workout" actually involves work, as well as being outside. The garden tones different muscles than the machines—shoveling pumps up my shoulders, for instance, while bending and twisting seem to trim the waist—although my abs will always resemble a keg as opposed to a six-pack. There is no doubt that seeing the fruits of one's labor actually turn into fruit makes the work, as the Marxists like to say, less alienating. The only thing I've ever grown while working out indoors on the ski machine is a fungus so bad I had to use Cruex to stop the jock itch.

Because the garden is one of the few places in modern society where you can do whatever you want.

Cut down a tree in your backyard that's too close to the

marsh and you're in the cross hairs of the conservation commission. Shoot an intruder in your home and it's you who are in trouble with the law. Just try to turn your garage into an extra bedroom without a building permit. But who gives a damn what you do in the garden? Bulldoze your roses and booby trap your hillside with yucca. Buzz cut your lawn till it looks like a billiard table. You like cement buddhas? A twelve-foot tall statue of the goddess Minerva made of welded oil drums? Every Halloween where I live a woman populates her lawn with an army of life-size ghouls, six-foot figurines holding rubber daggers, blood-soaked corpses and marching zombies, stopping traffic for miles. A ridiculous garden is one of the only things you can do on your own property that is not against the law. Feel free to express your bad taste. People will snicker but secretly love you. It makes them feel superior. It gives entire families a destination, someplace to drive past and ridicule instead of each other on long holiday weekends.

Because the garden makes you a philanthropist.

Back in the last decade of the twentieth century people thought writers made a lot of money. They thought that because they had seen a good review of a book in the *New York Times*, and a stack of them in the bookstore window, people were actually buying those books. I remember counting a writer friend's money when a book of hers landed on the *New York Times* bestseller list. I remember doing a kind of hallucinatory calculus, pulling a royalty rate out of nowhere, like, say, 10% of the catalog retail price, and multiplying it by a phantasmagorical number of copies, like, say, 300,000, and figuring that my friend had suddenly received a check for a million dollars. These days it's well documented that only a small number of titles get bought by a large number of people and that most writers don't make much money at all. It's a drag but at least our friends no longer make up fantasies about us. Never mind. We have vegetables.

In June we have enough lettuce to confidently stock every salad bar south of Boston, Massachusetts. This crop is immediately followed by long glossy rows of spinach plants with leaves as large as the ears of green elephants. It takes approximately half a station wagon full of fresh spinach to make one pound frozen, six hundred gallons of water to wash every pound and four hours of labor per. As we dedicate at least a week of our lives to freezing spinach we figure each pound to be worth about $85. Now that climate change has bumped us up to Zone 7 we have broccoli at the same time but after two weeks of eating it every day for lunch and dinner and in breakfast omelets with cheese, there are still so many heads going to flower that we put up vast tubs of broccoli soup. I forgot to mention the snow peas. And zucchini, which are famously prolific: even novice gardeners have getting-rid-of-zucchini stories. Personally I keep a database of people who do not have gardens—working mothers with young children, people confined to wheel chairs, anyone who owns a boat—which is what makes carrots so nice and leeks, which likewise can stay in the ground for months, like friends who don't demand attention but are there when you need them. The tomatoes are painfully slow to arrive. Most of the college freshmen in the United States have already hauled their TVs, DVD players, laptops, refrigerators, crock-pots, and microwave ovens into their dorm rooms before we get our first tomato. The early ones are round red miracles anticipated like the first grandchild. The rest descend like quintuplets. We freeze them, puree them, can them, dry them, squeeze them into juice. We make chutney, hot sauce, spaghetti sauce, ketchup, soup. We barter them for lobsters, quahogs, little necks, blue fish, striped bass, oysters and the promise of chainsaw work come hurricane season. We FedEx tomatoes to my wife's literary agent, who gives me the run of her swank Upper East Side apartment when I need to stay in New York City. But mostly we give them away by the bushel. In August we are the MacArthur Foundation of vegetables, bestowing grants, as the Foundation itself advertises, "on talented individuals who have shown extraordinary originality and dedication in their creative pursuits and a marked capacity for self-direction," i.e., our friends. This is as close as we come to knowing what it's like to be rich.

Because gardening equals sex.

I don't know if alfalfa farmers scuttle from their combines with a stiffy and meet in the barn for a quick one before lunch. It's hard to imagine the old couple in Grant Wood's *American Gothic* ever headed for bed after an afternoon harvesting garlic. But we do. I do not know why this is true but gardening makes us hot. My wife maintains that women are turned on by watching men fix things. However many times I've benefited from this peculiar chromosomal disorder, I find it difficult to imagine wanting to jump the plumber's bones. For my part I only know that working the dirt takes my mind off my worries, the bills, and politics. I know I like to watch the sweat drip down the small of her back when she's kneeling over tomato transplants. I know that as the daylight slowly increases after a dark New England winter, desire fills the pores of my body like sap and we both come alive to each other as the ground thaws and the wind carries the faint scent of new growth.

I know it's the opposite of the way romance is sold, with lithe slender bodies and enticing smiles. In the garden you get filthy, your face is caked with sweat, your muscles ache. You've tromped through manure, hauled a hundred-pound cartload of salt-marsh hay. You're as much a farm animal as a human being. So what is it about working in the garden together all afternoon that makes us both want to fuck? I don't know, frankly. It's a mystery. One I enjoy too much to care to solve.

The producer arrived in a rented Land Rover. She wore a Burberry safari jacket and knee-high pirate boots with stiletto heels. Although I gave her a hearty wave from the top of the driveway she did not leave the front seat of her vehicle but kept peering perplexedly at her map as if having set out for a country estate and arriving at a pig farm.

As soon as she stepped out of her vehicle she began sneezing, slapping at imagined mosquitoes, and rooting through her purse for a handkerchief, which she plastered to her face as if preparing to wade through a roomful of smoke. Upon seeing the house she made a desperate run for the front door, her long thin heels getting stuck in the mud.

Once inside she begged me to lock down the windows and turn on the air conditioner. Composing herself with a cup of tea and a handful of pills from an array of pharmacy bottles, she managed a few words of conversation. "You live here *all* year?" as if taking stock of a deep dark well she had fallen into.

I explained what I loved about country life, the slow passage of time, the privilege of living amongst other species, the essential tension between humanity and nature, and above all, and here I drew her to the window, to the pleasure I got from the garden.

She nodded as if indulging a madman and took a long deep restorative breath of air-conditioned air.

But I couldn't help apologizing. "Of course, at this time of year, with the wet weather, weeds are inevitable."

Like a victim forced to humor her tormentor, she forced a short, measured look before turning her back. "Oh, yes. They are very nice."

Six weeks later I was fired, replaced by another screen-writer. My agent insisted they loved me, loved the project, but wanted to go in a different direction. She reminded me that Hollywood was all about relationships and that I had to think long term. There were too many coincidences in the second act, the producer had told her. The hero's arc wasn't fully developed. But I will go to my grave wondering if it wasn't the weeds.

YOU ARE WHAT YOU OWE

Now I had proof. I was not paranoid. Here it was, exposed in black and white, what every writer knew deep down but didn't dare to think.

The article, in the newsletter of the National Writers Union, reported on an agent following up on a manuscript he'd sent an editor. The editor said that he liked the book well enough but asked, "What's the author like?"

"She's blonde, she's 30 years old and she's adorable," the agent said and within a week the editor made an offer for the book.

Even famous writers, no matter how many books they've written or great reviews they've received, secretly feel like starter wives, fearful of being replaced in their publisher's eyes by the next big talent, the new young thing. When I was 35, my own first novel was published to wonderful attention. My publisher was ecstatic. "You're hot!" But not for long. Like the freshman girl who did it under the bleachers with the captain of the football team, I couldn't even get him to return my calls.

Sooner or later every writer I know decides he can do a better job than his publisher. I have a friend who was one of America's best-selling authors, an Oprah's Book Club Choice. But when his books started selling thousands of copies instead of hundreds of thousands, he concluded his publisher was at fault. Reading a few how-to books written by former publishing industry publicists, he hired his own former publishing industry publicist to devise a marketing plan that his publishers might have come up with had they not been preoccupied by the new young thing on their list whose work was more "commercial"—a category of books that is anathema to serious writers unless it is used to describe their own.

I too thought I could do it better than my publisher. This is largely why I became a publisher. I had a business plan and a mission statement and above all the determination to treat writers with respect. I prepared for two years, telling everyone I knew that I could do it better than my publisher, reading every book I could find by former publishing industry publicists, interviewing publishers large and small, those who worked out of swank Manhattan offices and those who used an old barn as a warehouse; some who had entered the business with a strong literary vision and others who simply published books they liked. The New York publishers were cynical about the future of the book business. They trotted out the usual suspects, the chains, the electronic media, the decline in literacy, and fondly reminisced about the years of six-figure advances and three-hour lunches. I asked one legendary editor how he saw himself in the changing milieu. "Once," he said, "I felt like I was playing center field for the Yankees and now I'm Dilbert." But I pressed on, pigeonholing anyone who had something to teach me and ten minutes to spare, searching for my own quiet corner of the book world and finding it in the midst of all-out chaos.

Book Expo America is a bloated media carnival of high tech booths and hyperbolic lit buzz, the largest book trade show in the world, the NASCAR of belles-lettres, a writhing monkey barrel of marketing professionals climbing over each other for attention. Indoor skyscrapers of polyurethane tubing frame pavilions as long as football fields with turf of plush red carpet. Backlit blowups of book jackets and writers with palsied smiles line the aisles like posters in a freak show midway. Librarians, booksellers, critics, authors, bloggers, and bobbing throngs of bookbiz junketeers push folding carts full of posters, baseball caps, tote bags, beach balls, ballpoints, t-shirts, mouse pads, and every manner of promo crap ever shipped out of the People's Republic of China. Bill Clinton signs books for a line of fans a quarter of a mile long. Richard Simmons in purple velvet running shorts does jumping jacks in the aisle. Strippers in pink satin garter belts hawk a celebrity madam tell-all in a mock nineteenth-century brothel erected next to a fifty-foot-high Lego display. Three-hundred-pound Dixieland musicians wearing Hawaiian leis play the Muskrat Ramble while an Elvis imitator fumbles with the crotch of his rhinestone jump suit and poses for a snapshot with the assistant manager of a Barnes & Noble from Erie, Pennsylvania.

But far from the stacks of advance reading copies doled out by young publicity assistants in tight pin-stripe pantsuits, beyond the sleek gray-carpeted booths of the academic presses and the garish hawkers of book-store novelties, through the double doors of the satellite convention hall, to the right of the rest rooms and the left of the five-dollar-pretzel vendor, are the aisles of the independent publishers. Foot traffic is slower here, the lighting subdued, the freebies modest, the visitors cautious. They are offering penny candy here, post cards, book marks, bound galleys with titles promising sex and revolution. Their covers show full frontal nudes, brown-skinned peoples carrying rifles, a headshot of a gallant young Noam Chomsky. A librarian from Little Rock making her way from the ladies' room peers warily up the aisle. The owner of an Annie's Book Swap in western Massachusetts who spent all morning filling his cart with give-away books to sell back at the store furtively grabs a copy of *Going Down: Perfecting the Art of a Good Blowjob.*

While the New York publishers wore suits from Barney's and Prada loafers, this was a dress-down world of turtlenecks and sneakers, peasant skirts and motorcycle boots, prideful independents who sneered at the conglomerate giants. Literature was paramount; money beside the point. I had finally found my people. Or so I imagined.

Obscured by my romantic delusions was the fact that while the most cynical of these crusading independents were indeed strapped for cash, others were backed by an invisible fortune. The white-haired old hippie in John Lennon-style sunglasses was financed by an heiress who pumped seed money into any press that published her books. The overfed media hound dressed head to toe in black leather was the son of a world famous politician. A psychiatrist who left his practice after amassing a huge portfolio; the heir to a Brazilian industrial fortune (whom I had thought hearing impaired until I understood he had so much money there was no one he need listen to); a fundraising savant who played the foundations like a pinball wizard; the third son of the fourteenth Earl of Cricklade, simply had more to fall back on than book sales. I summoned the courage to ask the advice of an infamous counter culture publisher whose company had survived for decades and introduced some of America's best known authors—all of whom had gone on to publish with New York presses after making it big. A hulking bear of a man who wore an old flannel shirt and a leather sheath with a long hunting knife, he dropped a thick calloused hand on my shoulder and said, "Friend, you are what you owe."

Having been inculcated by my forebears with a fear of

debt in any form, mortgages, bank loans, car payments—when my grandfather took his extended family out once a year to Ratner's, a dairy restaurant on Delancey Street, he paid the check *before* we ate—I continued my research with less enthusiasm. But by now my wife had grown exasperated and committed us to a point of no return, writing a letter to twenty-five well-known writer friends asking them to recommend manuscripts. Once the post office box began to fill there was no turning back.

I was obsessed with appearing legitimate. Who was I to claim to be a publisher? Why would critics review our books? Why would bookstores carry them? Did it matter that the title page of our books located us in a tiny Massachusetts fishing village rather than a big city? What would happen if agents found out our office was a one-room winter rental with no heat? I invented an editorial staff and put their bios on the website, hip young ivy-league grads in their twenties with cool names. Elvis Kahn was my favorite. He rose from the ranks of editorial assistant to acquisitions editor and was the point man for many negotiations, an amusing situation until I was asked to lunch by a book page editor with whom I had been talking via telephone, as Elvis, for over a year. But first and foremost was the mission to support writers.

When we first started the press we were so dedicated that we would read every submission that arrived—sometimes all the way through!—and write two-page letters full of editing suggestions. Soon word got out: we were the best place in the country to get rejected.

Even if they don't publish your book, they critique it! The slush pile grew to the height of a refrigerator and if you caught sight of it in just the wrong light it seemed to have eyes and fangs and sneer at you like the Thurber cartoon of a house morphed into an angry woman's face. It took me years to get Marge to stop reading every page of every book in the slush pile. I learned my own lesson after throwing a manuscript across the room.

It was late, I was tired, glossing over it in that kind of numb state in which you follow the credits of a movie when I realized it was not an erotic novel I was holding in my hands, but puerile, fetishistic pornography about red welts on bare buttocks and little girls' panties and pee, the infantile fantasy of a stunted child-man's mind. Nor did I pick up the pages but swept them into a plastic garbage bag. As the address on the return envelope was from a nearby town and I imagined being stalked for a reply, I scribbled, "Sorry, we don't publish this sort of thing," taped it closed in lieu of licking it and washed my hands. Some days later I received an e-mail reply from the writer, "Thank you, Ira, for being so nice."

Having been a writer before I was a publisher doomed me to be nice, like a former waiter compelled to over-tip. Only once in ten years do I remember losing it, doing something blatantly nasty to a writer we published. Here was a guy whose career we had saved, who, if not dead in the water when he approached us, had a lot of trouble placing his work.

He had had one groundbreaking book that had been

a bestseller and many afterwards that sold in diminishing numbers. But he was a tireless self-promoter. He had a cable TV chat show, he hosted a reading series, he collected favors, he schmoozed. He submitted a novel that was almost published by a prestigious New York press, almost, but was missing something that no editor was able to pinpoint. If our little press, stranded on outermost Cape Cod, having upgraded its corporate headquarters to a grain warehouse with no windows, had proved itself adept at anything it was the resurrection of near misses: diagnosing the need for a new beginning, a tighter plot, a selling title; a publicity hook or simply an understanding of the mood of the country. (One of our most successful titles, a west coast bestseller, was rejected in New York during the early Bush years because no editor there could imagine that a hilarious comedy about a gay Jewish liberal trapped in a fundamentalist bible college could find a market.) The book by the self-promoter enjoyed respectable advance sales. The author and I spent a year together on editing and promotion; we were text messaging every day.

OUTBOX: LAT revu sched for 12/1.

INBOX: ^5! U d'man!

But after awhile we began to spat like rock musicians cooped up together on a thirty-city tour, or more accurately, like a married couple, each member of which feels his or her work is invisible to the other.

INBOX: ??? Did U call Union SQ B&N to gt me rdg there?

OUTBOX: Only 300 times.

Expectations are high in publishing. It's difficult for an author to understand why he wasn't reviewed in the *New York Times*, or why his recent books fizzle when his first did well. Or why a book about an unrepentant shop-aholic or an un-trainable dog gets a lot of attention while an insightful family character study is all but neglected. A writer can blame himself, of course, but what did he do except sacrifice four years of his life to hard work and research? Sooner or later most writers start to think they can do a better job than their publisher.

When I started to receive daily e-mails demanding that I resubmit his book to critics who had declined to review it, when he accused me of spending more time and money on another author's book, I sent him a rotten *Kirkus*.

Kirkus was one of the most esteemed of the advance trade reviews, those magazines that critique books two to three months before they are made available for sale. A really good *Kirkus* can generate a rush of calls from movie producers; a bad one means surprisingly little. Except to an author. A bad *Kirkus*, with its razor sharp invective, can signal the arrival of Armageddon to an author who has been waiting years for the public's response. Most publishers are disappointed by an unfavorable *Kirkus* and simply file it away. But I figured a little humility was in order here and I duly faxed it on. Our relations were noticeably more cordial after that and have been ever since.

Although publishers large and small delegate their slush piles to the lowliest dogsbodies in the organization, they're usually too superstitious to disregard them entirely, and do read them, however slowly and partially, because they always have the nagging fear that they might be rejecting a work of genius. *War and Peace*, *Remembrance of Things Past*, *To Kill a Mockingbird*, were all rejected by publishers. Some nitwit even passed on the *Joy of Cooking*. We found one of our most successful books through the slush pile. It was brilliant, original, topical and scholarly; Marge had selected it out of hundreds of manuscripts and kept hounding me to read it. Once I did I called the author immediately but by that time he was dead. We had missed him by three weeks. We couldn't tell the widow we weren't going to publish her husband's magnum opus but we weren't keen on the book's chances. We had nobody to send on tour, nobody to do interviews, no future young talent for the media to discover. In despair I turned to the publicist of one of the country's most successful literary publishers. "Oh, Ira, don't be discouraged," she said. "Dead authors can be great to work with." Better, sad to say, than some live ones.

While the dead author's book caught a huge break, hailed by the press as the second coming of *A Confederacy of Dunces*—the posthumous comic novel that won its author a Pulitzer Prize—I encountered a number of authors who promised to help promote their titles but, once the book was accepted, had no intention of following through.

It's disheartening when a writer turns out to have stage fright and gives a terrible performance. We published a photogenic young woman who looked like sex itself in a black leather mini-skirt but who mumbled through her first chapter at a bookstore appearance as if listing a prescription drug's side effects on a radio commercial. There's no way of telling who can perform and who cannot. I conversed for a year via telephone with an articulate novelist whom we arranged to have read at a book festival. I knew him only from his publicity headshot and didn't recognize him at the airport. Far from the dashing outdoorsman with a salt-and-pepper beard and a lecherous twinkle in his eye, he stumbled into the baggage claim area like an elderly Walt Whitman and in fact read like Whitman himself, recorded in 1890 on an Edison wax cylinder. An author doesn't have to be a great performer. She can develop a fan base in a blog, review books on the radio. But some authors, many of whom are academics, view a new book as a bullet point in their resume and their publisher as something like the department secretary.

My least favorite author—the one who was less helpful than the dead one, and here I am going to take pains to conceal his identity, so let's call him Errol Schmuck—refused not only to make author appearances without being paid, but also to proofread his book. "Man, I'm a poet, I'm not into this proofreading jive and besides, I've got finals to grade." Proofreading your manuscript, as every writer knows, is an important thing to do, perhaps especially so for poetry. Poets use so few words to say so much that each word carries more weight than that of a work of prose. Only the poet knows the precise rhythm and punctuation and break in the line; no copy editor can verify what is intended. So a poet, of all writers, needs to be the one to make the final judgment on the manuscript. But Errol Schmuck had finals to grade and did not catch the elimination of a page break that resulted in the fusing of two poems.

The reviews, I'm happy to say, were splendid. Apparently, nobody noticed. Except Errol Schmuck, who demanded a nationwide recall. We placed an errata sheet in the small first printing, offered to exchange all misprinted copies for a new one, and immediately ran a corrected second printing. End of story.

Not quite. The first telephone call came at midnight. Although I wasn't in the office to answer, I was able to savor it and all those that followed on the answering machine, counting the many ways you can call someone a cheap Jew without actually saying it. I sort of enjoyed the subsequent series of blistering e-mails we exchanged but not the calls from booksellers who wanted to know what to do about the broad-shouldered, very angry man who planted himself at the check-out counter with an armful of books from their shelves, claiming that he was the author, that the books were "tainted" and that he demanded they be returned to the publisher. Yes, of course, we accepted them. I then paid the distributor to comb through every last book in the warehouse. For years the notice on our website read: "You may be in possession of a book with a serious error. This is a rare book and may be of considerable value to collectors. We will gladly exchange it for a corrected copy from a subsequent printing." We never had a taker, not one.

Before I began the press I imagined publishers who wore wide wale corduroys and French blue shirts with flamboyant bow ties, who worked late into the night blue-penciling manuscripts, then went for martinis with starry-eyed young women editors to whom they were legends. I didn't own a blue pencil, but I did wear corduroys, and a sweater and a muffler, and I did work late into the night reading manuscripts next to the space heater in my office, willing them to captivate me with the same plaintive longing with which I stared into the refrigerator at lunch time, as if simply looking long and hard enough would give rise to something I could actually eat, or in this case, sell.

Why, I wondered, had I ever wanted to sell books instead of write them? It wasn't that people didn't love books and want to read them, they just didn't see why they should buy them retail. And why would they when new books were free in libraries and used ones selling for pennies online? Sometimes, as the wind shook the old wooden building and the clock ticked to daybreak, as the reality of money and sales or, to be honest, the lack of both, kept me up at night, my catastrophic mind set loose, I imagined thousands of unsold books returning to our warehouse from bookstores all over America—on pallets, in boxes, on trucks, in trains, mounting in piles like the columns of debt in my monthly statements. In an effort to soothe myself to sleep I made lists, conjuring all the things that were easier to sell than books—pizza, tattoos, t-shirts. One night I imagined standing on a street corner hawking underpants, a ridiculous comparison but one that in my increasingly battered frame of mind deserved scrutiny. People *needed* underpants. Most people did not feel they *needed* a book. Nor were critics likely to write a sarcastic review of a pair of underpants. And who would ever pass a pair of old underpants to a friend—"Have you worn this? I think you'll enjoy it."—or sell it to a used underwear dealer? But most shameful was the way I began to feel about books, once a treasured source of knowledge and delight, now a symbol of failure and pain.

One day, however, I received a telephone call from a starry-eyed young woman editor to whom I was apparently a legend. Her voice was hesitant. "I'm so sorry to interrupt you but I . . . me and my backers, that is . . . are starting a small press." Recalling my own timid questions at BEA and the publishers who took the time to answer them I invited her to my office.

"We l-o-v-e your press," she said upon driving two hours to get here and shyly admitted she was copying our website design, our mission statement, the "look" of our books. "You're so cool," she said, "so cutting edge."

She picked my brain for details I had forgotten years ago and I had to admit to an unexpected *frisson*, the attentions of a cute young woman who saw in me everything

I had wanted to become. But surrounded by stacks of titles we had published, giant blow-ups of book covers, boxes of promotional rubber toys, a six-foot-long calendar board that projected the deadline of every task for the next twelve months, she found herself in paradise while I was in a prison of my own making. At one time in my life a situation such as this, a bright and energetic young woman who was asking for my guidance might have led me to fantasize one scenario while I was already beginning to conjure another. After several more meetings I was ready to make my move.

I proposed a small café this time, unhurried and intimate, and found a table where we would not be overheard. When she entered, late and sweetly frazzled as always, she didn't see me at first but glowed as soon as we locked eyes. When she sat down I admitted I'd been thinking a lot about her. She blushed. "But," I edged closer and said in a hesitant whisper, "there's something we need to talk about."

She looked wary.

"Promise me you'll think it over, that you won't just say no."

Now I was beginning to freak her out but before she could answer, I came out with it: "I think you should buy the company."

"What?"

"You promised me you'd think about it."

"I did not."

"That you wouldn't just say no."

"I don't have that kind of money."

"You have backers."

"But we can't afford to buy a publishing company."

"How do you know? Do you have any idea how much you'll need to start one? How many years it takes to develop a brand? How many books you'll have to publish before you attract a distributor? Wouldn't your backers rather take over a ten-year-old company with a great national reputation than start from scratch?"

"But the financing."

"Leave the financing to me. I'll come up with something you can manage."

"I doubt that."

"Trust me. I can."

There were lawyers involved, money to raise, a contract with endless terms. We went back and forth for almost a year. Some days it seemed a deal was likely to happen; others it appeared impossible. But we persevered, pestering people for advice, looking for likely models, studying endless options—much as I had done years before—she for the dream of owning a publishing company and me to get out from under one.

When the deal was actually done I was in uncertain territory. I no longer quite knew how to define or what to do with myself. Having made lists of all the projects I couldn't wait to begin I was positively featherbrained and unable to focus for months. A famous episode from the Oprah show kept running through my mind, the one in which she dragged a red wagon full of suet on

201

stage to symbolize the weight she'd lost. For the first time in ten years I felt free, free of debt and deadlines and the slush pile; free to read once again for pleasure. The book business and all the expectations I carried around had been my red wagon full of fat. I didn't know if I wanted to write again and if I did I would never quite look at editors the same way. For having spent a decade acquiring, editing, designing, and selling books, I attained a certain insight into the secret desires of those who publish them. Far from wanting to replace their writers with new young talent, many publishers have a more personal agenda, a longing few writers imagine: If I didn't have all this contractual, marketing, and publicity crap to take care of, Hell, I could write a book and do it *better* than my authors.

THE SECOND MARSHMALLOW: AN EPILOGUE

My father once stared at me for a few long moments before expressing something that he seemed to have just figured out. "You know, you can talk to anyone in the world for half an hour."

It might have been when I was visiting the family in Lynchburg, Virginia, or Savannah, Georgia, or Miami Beach, any one of the cities to which they moved and kept moving as the clothing trade moved south. There was always a pool at the apartment complexes where they lived and around the pool, strangers; all their old friends and relatives left behind. Since on these visits I usually passed a lot of time talking with whoever was around, this is where I remember the conversation happening. When I understood that he had actually taken notice of this practice of mine, I would engage absolutely anyone in his presence: neighbors, deliverymen, his colleagues from work. It didn't matter. It was something that my dad admired.

As difficult as a facility for wanton conversation must have seemed to a shy man like my father, it was surprisingly easy, in fact a necessity, for those of us for whom silence in the presence of strangers feels impossibly awkward. Although peppering people with questions, telling jokes, making small talk about children or gardens or sports was a habit that served me well on dates and at parties and the like, it drove my wife crazy when I first met her and she did her best to help me curb the impulse. I can still feel it coming on. I can feel myself beginning to entertain people waiting in line at movie theaters. I have to stop myself from jabbering with cab drivers, UPS guys, the plumber at 90 dollars an hour. The willpower to remain silent while staring at the ceiling with my mouth open wide and not to engage the woman who cleans my teeth is almost impossible to muster.

Although a quick glance at any early photograph of myself is all the evidence I need to confirm I am no longer the person in these stories, the impulses of the past, even the distant past, remain. Sometimes I think of them as a phantom limb. Decades removed, they still tingle and twitch.

I've come to think that it's the ability to deny these impulses that sets our early selves apart from the people we've grown to become. A psychologist named Walter Mischel once offered a large plate of marshmallows to a group of preschool kids at Stanford University. He told them they could eat one marshmallow immediately, but they could eat two if they waited for him to return from doing an errand. After fourteen years of following data on their lives he discovered that the kids who were able to deny the impulse to eat the marshmallow had better SAT scores, were happier, and were better adjusted.

All but one of the stories in this collection re-play the memories of a man who lived them decades ago. I don't remember the last time I was even in the same room with a gram of cocaine and have certainly never done a line of it since. But I still sometimes long for the obliteration of the inner censor and the sublime illusion that whatever I've written is a triumph of the imagination. I was re-elected to office three times since my first disastrous term as a Selectman. I had to train myself not to personalize issues. I had to learn not to befriend town employees however many times the impulse to do so returned. Nor do I get jealous of the success of others. I might experience a stab of envy when a friend receives a great review, but I've learned to put it in context. Given the disappearance of so many independent newspapers today, that great review is likely one of very few he's received. Most miraculously, after thirty-six years, I am still very happily married to her. However many years it has taken, I have learned to wait for the second marshmallow.

Still, the strongest of the impulses somehow win out. Like my mania for talking. I still do it, in a studio, on public radio, every week. Call me.

THE AUTHOR

Ira Wood is the author of three novels, *The Kitchen Man,* *Going Public,* and *Storm Tide*, co-authored by Marge Piercy, with whom he has also written *So You Want to Write: How to Master the Craft of Writing Fiction and Memoir.* They make their home on four acres of land in a small fishing village on Cape Cod. His talk show, *The Lowdown,* addresses politics, books, and national trends. It airs on WOMR-FM Provincetown, a Pacifica network affiliate, and streams worldwide on WOMR. ORG. His website is irawood.com.

About the Type

This book was set in Adobe Garamond.

Claude Garamond (ca. 1480–1561) cut types for the Parisian scholar-printer Robert Estienne in the first part of the sixteenth century, basing his romans on the types cut by Francesco Griffo for Venetian printer Aldus Manutius in 1495. After his death in 1561, the Garamond punches made their way to the printing office of Christoph Plantin in Antwerp, where they were used by Plantin for many decades, and still exist in the Plantin-Moretus museum. Italics for Garamond fonts were cut by Robert Granjon (1513–1589), who worked for Plantin.

Adobe Garamond™ was designed by Robert Slimbach in 1989. The roman weights were based on the true Garamond, and the italics on those of punchcutter Robert Granjon.

Designed by John Taylor-Convery
Composed at JTC Imagineering, Santa Maria, CA